Bibl...
...

Since 2007 the Biblioa... ...ranslation Series has been publishing exciting literature from Europe, Latin America, Africa and the minority languages of Canada. Committed to the idea that translations must come from the margins of linguistic cultures as well as from the power centres, the Biblioasis International Translation Series is dedicated to publishing world literature in English in Canada. The editors believe that translation is the lifeblood of literature, that a language that is not in touch with other linguistic traditions loses its creative vitality, and that the worldwide spread of English makes literary translation more urgent now than ever before.

1. *I Wrote Stone: The Selected Poetry of Ryszard Kapuściński* (Poland)
Translated by Diana Kuprel and Marek Kusiba

2. *Good Morning Comrades*
by Ondjaki (Angola)
Translated by Stephen Henighan

3. *Kahn & Engelmann*
by Hans Eichner (Austria-Canada)
Translated by Jean M. Snook

4. *Dance with Snakes*
by Horacio Castellanos Moya (El Salvador)
Translated by Lee Paula Springer

5. *Black Alley*
by Mauricio Segura (Quebec)
Translated by Dawn M. Cornelio

6. *The Accident*
by Mihail Sebastian (Romania)
Translated by Stephen Henighan

7. *Love Poems*
by Jaime Sabines (Mexico)
Translated by Colin Carberry

8. *The End of the Story*
by Liliana Heker (Argentina)
Translated by Andrea G. Labinger

9. *The Tuner of Silences*
by Mia Couto (Mozambique)
Translated by David Brookshaw

10. *For as Far as the Eye Can See*
by Robert Melançon (Quebec)
Translated by Judith Cowan

11. *Eucalyptus*
by Mauricio Segura (Quebec)
Translated by Donald Winkler

12. *Granma Nineteen and the Soviet's Secret*
by Ondjaki (Angola)
Translated by Stephen Henighan

13. *Montreal Before Spring*
by Robert Melançon (Quebec)
Translated by Donald McGrath

14. *Pensativities: Essays and Provocations*
by Mia Couto (Mozambique)
Translated by David Brookshaw

15. *Arvida*
by Samuel Archibald (Quebec)
Translated by Donald Winkler

16. *The Orange Grove*
by Larry Tremblay (Quebec)
Translated by Sheila Fischman

Arvida

SAMUEL ARCHIBALD
ARVIDA
Stories

TRANSLATED FROM THE FRENCH BY
DONALD WINKLER

BIBLIOASIS
WINDSOR, ONTARIO

Originally published as *Arvida: histoires* by Le Quartanier, Montreal, 2011.

Author photo © Le Quartanier / Frédérick Duchesne
Copyright © Samuel Archibald, 2015
Translation copyright © Donald Winkler, 2015

FIRST EDITION
Third printing, October 2015

Library and Archives Canada Cataloguing in Publication

Archibald, Samuel, 1978-
[Arvida. English]
    Arvida / Samuel Archibald ; translated by Donald Winkler.

Translation of: Arvida.
Short stories.
ISBN 978-1-77196-042-7 (paperback)

    I. Winkler, Donald, translator II. Title. III. Title: Arvida.
English.

PS8601.R39A7513 2015   C843'.6   C2015-903738-7

Biblioasis acknowledges the ongoing financial support of the Government of Canada through the Canada Council for the Arts, Canadian Heritage, the Canada Book Fund; and the Government of Ontario through the Ontario Arts Council and the Ontario Media Development Corporation. Biblioasis also acknowledges the financial support of the Government of Canada through the National Translation Program for Book Publishing, an initiative of the *Roadmap for Canada's Official Languages 2013–2018: Education, Immigration, Communities*, for our translation activities.

Edited by Stephen Henighan
Copy-edited by Allana Amlin
Cover designed by Kate Hargreaves and Chris Andrechek
Typeset by Chris Andrechek

PRINTED AND BOUND IN CANADA

MIX
Paper from
responsible sources
FSC® C004071

CONTENTS

My Father and Proust ARVIDA I   9

Antigonish   17

Cryptozoology   27

In the Midst of the Spiders   49

América   57

In the Fields of the Lord BLOOD SISTERS I   69

A Mirror in the Mirror   77

The Animal BLOOD SISTERS II   85

自害 (Jigai)   109

Paris in the Rain BLOOD SISTERS III   127

The Centre of Leisure and Forgetfulness ARVIDA II   137

The Last-Born   159

House Bound   171

Madeleines ARVIDA III   203

My Father and Proust
ARVIDA I

MY GRANDMOTHER, mother of my father, often said:

"There are no thieves in Arvida."

For a long time, it's true, there were only good people in Arvida. Honest and industrious Catholics, and the Protestant owners and managers of the aluminum plant, who were basically, if you could believe my father, good human beings. You could leave your tools lying around in the garage. You could leave car doors unlocked and house doors open.

There was a very beautiful photo from after the war, which was, like all beautiful photos, an empty picture, with practically nothing in it and everything outside it. In it, a dozen bicycles were strewn over the lawn in front of the clinic. Outside the photo, in the building's basement, children were lined up before a large white curtain, waiting to be vaccinated against polio. Outside the photo, the few times I saw it, my grandmother pressed her finger down on it, saying:

"You see? There are no thieves in Arvida."

That's what she said all her life, my grandmother, mother of my father. Except for about twenty years when, from time to time, she looked at my father and said:

"There were no thieves in Arvida. Now there's you."

★

It's true that almost all the family stories relating to my father were tales of larceny. Including the very first. At the age of three my father was overwhelmed for the very first time by desire for the giant May Wests beckoning from the baker's basket. They were called *Mae Wests* then, after the actress. Vachon kept this spelling until Mae West's estate sent them a legal letter, in 1980. May Wests cost five cents, and the family budget did not allow for this kind of extravagance. After being told no by his mother a good dozen times, my father decided to change his strategy.

A bit later that year, my Aunt Lise received fifteen cents from her godmother Monique for her birthday. One morning, while his mother was dealing with the baker, my father entered the girls' room and stole the money from their chest of drawers. He went downstairs on tiptoe, snuck outside without his mother seeing, and hid behind a tree. When the baker went to get back in his truck, my father came out of hiding and intercepted him, hanging onto his legs.

He opened his hand and held out fifteen cents.

"My mother forgot to give you this."

"What for?"

"Some May Wests."

"What you have there would give you three big May Wests."

"It was my birthday this week."

"How old are you?"

"Ten."

The baker knew perfectly well that my father was lying about his age and everything else. But he'd seen the little man drooling over his basket for so long that he didn't want to play the policeman. He sold him the cakes. My father went and hid himself away in the shadows under the porch. He crouched down among the dry leaves and the rotten boards along with the spiders and centipedes. In no time at all he devoured the

May Wests, taking huge mouthfuls, like a starving creature that had had nothing to eat all winter.

When his mother began calling him he went into the house, certain of having perpetrated the perfect crime, until she asked him why he had chocolate all over his face and even in his hair. He spent the entire afternoon in solitary confinement, and was freed only once, to give rein to a colossal diarrhea. So began a long series of weeks that my father spent in his penitential bedroom.

On another occasion, my grandmother had bought a box of factory-made cakes for Sunday supper. That seems a bit gauche today, to serve that kind of dessert to the whole family plus two or three priests. But it wasn't at the time, in the mid-sixties, when even in families as traditional as that of my grandparents there reigned a fascination for all things modern. It was a cardboard box with a diamond-shaped film of transparent plastic in the lower right corner, through which you could glimpse the whipped cream topping and little caramel coulis of a Saint-Joseph cake pre-cut into individual portions. Flushed with pride, my grandmother set the object down on the table and raised the lid, only to discover, at the same time as her guests, and to her own stupefaction, that the whole cake had been eaten except for the pitiful portion visible through the plastic. She might have torn my father limb from limb, but he had already fled, and was roaming the Arvida streets on his bicycle. As usual, when he knew that he wouldn't be leaving his room for quite a while, he rode very slowly through the town, taking in his favourite sights: the baseball park on Rue Castner, the two coulees where he went with his brothers to toss rocks at skunks, and the spacious no man's lands near the Alcan factory where he practised his golf shots. He gazed on them and touched them with his child's hands long enough to be able to inhabit them in his imagination during the weeks his sentence would last.

My father told dozens of stories like that. I thought for a long time that this litany of stolen treats and confiscated desserts had something Proustian about it.

Only later did I see how wrong I was.

When I was an adolescent myself, my father would sit at the head of the table and pass his time conveying an unlit cigarette from his mouth to a pristine ashtray. He drank a little wine, constantly refilling his half-empty glass. He didn't eat. He sat there, his legs crossed and his shoulders bowed, staring at us thoughtfully.

"You're not eating?" Nadia asked him.

"Eat. I'll eat afterwards."

When everyone had finished, he lit his cigarette. Often, he didn't eat at all. For a long time Nadia, my brother, and I, wondered why he did that. We couldn't explain it because Nadia was an excellent cook. The devil only knows if he did it on purpose, but my father contrived to have Nadia live her life surrounded by enough cooking pots for twenty grandmothers. It's often thought that men choose younger women so as not to have to deal with those who are mature. There's some truth in that, but real life has its way with these men just as it does with all others. In many respects, young women are the scourge God invented to punish men who prefer young women.[1]

Nadia was just out of adolescence when she became part of my father's life, and he himself was a belated adolescent of

---

[1] Laganière, an old friend of my brother, has cited my father as an example ever since he set his eyes, at the age of twenty-four, on a beauty from the Saguenay five years his junior. He likes to say to us (never in front of women, obviously), "Me, I saw Doug in action and I said to myself, 'There's a guy who's figured it all out.' Why weigh yourself down with an impossible woman and all her flaws when you can take one who's really young and mould her to your tastes before she's had time to develop a goddam nasty character?" My father always makes as if to accept the compliment, then he whispers in my ear, and that of my brother, "Poor imbecile. He doesn't know what's lying in wait for him."

thirty years and a bit, but over the years she became a woman, her own woman, very different from and often the diametric opposite of what my father would have wished her to be. But in the kitchen she was the amalgam of all the women my father had known. Who knows whether he'd planned it that way, but the evidence is there. Since he was small he'd always behaved as if he had a plan in mind. Whenever he ate something good, he showered his hostess with compliments, so as to get the recipe. My father knows that women accomplish and become what they want, but he also knows that at certain times women are not their own creatures, and that flattery is the best way to induce that state.

The devil only knows how he did it, but ten years after having met my father, Nadia had become a fabulous cook, haunted by the ghosts of dozens of women she had never known. She made extraordinarily good meals, and David and I told her so often, as did my father, after supper, walking the streets of Arvida.

"The first course was delicious."

"That was Mrs. Whitney's recipe. She was our neighbour when I was little, before Reynolds hired Mr. Whitney and they moved to Pittsburgh."

"And the main course?"

"Your grandmother's recipe."

"Your mother?"

"No. The mother of your mother. Éliane."

And yet, after the world had blessed him with the sum of all the cooks in his life, he sometimes never even touched his plate, or put anything on it. We saw this during the holidays, when I was visiting. I hadn't been back to Arvida very often since my leaving six years earlier, and I hadn't seen my father on a hunger strike for years. It may have been a reunion, but my father, at the head of the table, watched us eat in silence, sipping two fingers of wine from a water glass.

"Pa, aren't you eating?" asked my brother.

And that's when my father let it slip. He said:

"No, you eat. I'll eat what's left."

Nadia, David and I looked at each other. Smiling. Nadia's recipes were inspired for the most part by a time when people worked hard and families were big. She didn't know how to cook light and she didn't know how to cook for four. You could always find something in the kitchen, on the butcher's block and the counters, enough to feed my father's friends, my brother's and my friends, the scroungers and strays who turned up at our house any old time, most often just before dinner.

We finally understood. In the midst of all this abundance, the lasagnas, the roasts, the boeuf bourguignons only a third consumed, my father for ten years had been acting out a great comedy of privation, with himself in the role of the father sacrificing for his own. A comedy of abnegation set in a regimental mess.

When I think about it now, the comedy darkens. The more I age, the more something tragic makes its presence felt, the sense of a bitter nostalgia at the core of all things: the idea of wanting to do something magnanimous for people who ask for nothing and are in need of nothing; the idea of a sacrifice reduced to a risible and secret simulacrum; the idea that the object of desire has nothing to do with desire itself; the idea that the fulfillment of the desire never satisfies it, nor does it make it disappear, and that in the midst of all the things longed for desire survives in us, dwindling into remorse and regret.

My father no longer lacks for anything, but he misses the taste food had when there was not enough of it.

It's in pondering this that I understood that my father's childhood tales have nothing to do with Proust. They're even the polar opposite. In him, the deceptions, the gaffes, the misdemeanours and venial sins, the amorous thrills, the athletic exploits, everything, truly, in the end dwindles and melts away.

He told us how he saw people come out of their cars and throw up during a showing of *Jaws* at the Chicoutimi drive-in, and the story got side-tracked, lost itself in the odours of canteen grease and steamed hot-dogs.

He told us how Ghislaine, mother of the Devaux brothers, had been the first woman in Arvida to have breast implants inserted, early in the 1960s. After having seen a television report on the procedure, she had emptied her savings account and taken the only plane to Florida, saying to her husband Marcel:

"I've always liked that, big boobs."

We wanted to know how people had reacted, seeing her lissome silhouette deformed by twin mortars, a spectacular affront to the laws of gravity and good taste that she still flaunts in the summertime, slung high in her sweaters, at almost eighty years of age. Before getting that far my father more often than not strayed into a digression concerning the same Madame Devaux, who served him his first spaghetti bolognaise, a dish whose taste and texture he'd found unspeakably gross.

He often talked about the time he'd almost died on his way home from the sports centre. After a game, his hockey bag over his shoulder, famished, he'd swallowed a Cherry Blossom whole, biting into the chocolate and sucking on the syrup, while overlooking the maraschino cherry, which blocked his windpipe. He'd tried to breathe as best he could, feeling his strength wane and his mind lose focus, before giving up the ghost and letting himself drop onto a snowbank. The hard snow's impact expelled the cherry and sent it flying off into the grey sky before his clouded eyes. My father had lain there for a long time, numbed, before getting his breath back. We wanted to know what impact the incident had had on how he looked at life, but instead he chose to pronounce himself on Hershey Canada's buyout of Lowney's in 1952, and its inimical effect on the quality of a delicious chocolate that, to his mind, had become inedible.

If my father is a seasoned storyteller, food is his Achilles heel. For him, childhood does not spring full blown from a madeleine. On the contrary, all his childhood memories trail away into the evocation of a lost pastry and its indefinable flavour.

To truly understand what my father is talking about, you'd have to be able to savour a Sophie cake, a Saint-Joseph, or a big May West of yore, transforming a succession of vague metaphors into bodily stimuli. Phrases like "a chocolate that tasted equally of burnt coffee, cinnamon and *crème fraiche*" or "whipped cream icing with a hint of hazelnut and orange peel" strive to say something, but only to our minds, not our taste buds. The words taste of nothing. They accumulate in a long list of lost desserts, sketching out in thin restless lines the likeness of a penurious childhood.

There is no memory in our experience of things. Long lost pastries bring back childhood for ourselves alone, and even then, if we take the time to chew them as carefully as we should, we have to admit that they no longer taste the same.

Antigonish

AMERICA'S A BAD IDEA that's come a long way. I've always thought that, but it doesn't paint a very good picture.

I should have said: America's a bad idea that has gone every which way. An idea that's spawned endless roads leading nowhere, roads paved in asphalt or pounded into the earth or laid out with gravel and sand, and you can cruise them for hours to find pretty well zilch at the other end, a pile of wood, metal, bricks, and an old guy on his feet in the middle of the road, asking:

"Will you goddam well tell me what the hell you're doing around here?"

America is full of lost roads and places that really don't want anyone to get there. It took fools to make these roads and fools to live at the end of them, and there's no end of fools, but me, I'm another kind of fool, one of those who tries to reinvent history, pushing on to the very last road, and the very last god-forsaken destination.

I'm sure they've made a much more welcoming road now, with scenic walks and lookouts and all that stuff, but in those days, driving the Cabot Trail at night in the middle of a storm was a crazy idea. The guy at the Cape North gas bar had been polite enough not to say anything. He'd only said, "Drive fifteen, twenty miles an hour, no more, and God willing, you'll get to the other end."

I had a Ford Galaxy 500, 1966, with a Thunderbird V8 engine, 428 cubic inches, under the hood. It guzzled gas big time, that's for sure, and it gobbled up lots of asphalt, but that night it was rolling really slowly and nibbling away at increments of the road and the darkness and the fog that covered us and covered the trees, the cliffs, the Atlantic Ocean, and the whole world for all I knew.

Antigonish.

Menaud was sleeping beside me, so I couldn't tell him that the word made me think of Antigone, the daughter of the king of Thebes, and above all of *antagonist*, which was especially appropriate given that I was battling the Cabot Trail, tacking hard with the steering wheel and the wheels themselves. I probably wouldn't have let him in on that anyway. Menaud had the torso of a wrestler perched on bird feet, forearms like Popeye the sailor covered with long black hairs in zigzags, and between his incisors a hole big enough for you to poke in a finger. A thick beard lent a bluish cast to his neck and cheeks, and a single bushy eyebrow spawned a whole repertoire of grimaces where it overhung his evil eyes, hunched in their orbits like grackles in a stolen nest. He liked getting drunk, fighting in taverns, and telling stories he'd made up, and he'd never read a book in his life. We'd agreed, in '65, on our strange way of travelling, making as many miles as possible in the time we had, but after that I don't think we ever saw eye to eye on anything until in '68 Johnny Cash brought out the disc he'd recorded in Folsom Prison.

It was he, Menaud, who planned the trips. When he was fifteen, working on his father's farm, he'd decided to see the entire world. At eighteen he realized that he was subject to seasickness and afraid of flying. All he had left was America, if he wanted to satisfy his desire to see a world beyond the wide but constricted horizon of his agricultural land. The worst part was that he didn't even like to drive. He was the one who'd decided we'd take the Cabot Trail, and he'd decided we'd do it at night, and now he was snoring beside me with a bottle of Dow between his legs. He'd said:

"Seems you gotta see that."

I wondered what on earth he could see, spread-eagled on his seat with an arm across his face. Even with my eyes open, I could see almost nothing. A few feet of wet pavement in front of the headlights, and the pounding rain. The road was all ups and downs, in bends and twists, no more than an inch or two from the precipice. For most of the way I'd been driving by instinct, like blind creatures living in grottos and attics, sensing rather than seeing the forms things took in the rain.

I was half hypnotized when I saw her. She was standing by the side of the road wearing a short red coat, unfastened, over a big white dress. I barely saw her face, veiled by her black hair, very long, tossing in the wind. I was so numb that I kept going for a hundred more feet at least before putting on the brakes. It must have been pretty sudden, because Menaud woke up. He took a slug of beer.

"What's happening?"

"There's a girl back there, beside the road."

He turned his head, without really looking.

"You crazy?"

I sniffed, lit a cigarette, and opened my door. I said to Menaud:

"Wait here."

"I'm not waiting outside, that's for sure."

By the time I took three steps my clothes were soaked and my cigarette was out. I threw it onto the shoulder. The slope was steep enough that I had to brace my legs. I walked and walked, a lot farther than the spot where I'd seen the girl. And I didn't find her. I went back along the cliff, peering down at the rocks and the sea, two hundred feet below. I couldn't see much, and my clothes were now wet through. At one point I stopped and looked carefully, trying to pick out a form in the water or on the rocks. There was nothing, but I waited for a long time. The clouds were swollen with water, like the plastic sheets you hang up over drying wood, and they were full of electricity, too. I couldn't see well. I was dazzled by the lightning and blinded by its absence. I heard a din that was more like thunder than surf, I saw the waves crashing and exploding against the rocks in a commotion that had nothing gentle or harmonious about it, I saw the ocean like an immense black mass streaked with foam, and I understood that every time I'd seen the sea before that night, on the bridge of a ferry, at the lighthouse at Pointe-au-Père, or on the beach at Cape Cod, I'd seen a postcard, I'd seen a lie.

I went back to the car, running through the heavy rain. Menaud didn't ask me any questions and that suited me fine, because I wouldn't have known what to reply. By the time I'd calmed down and we were on our way, he'd gone back to sleep.

About four in the morning, I left the Cabot Trail for the 105, crossed from Cape Breton to mainland Nova Scotia through the Canso Canal and drove for a while on the 104.

A little after 4:30, I shook the dead weight next to me, and said:

"Menaud, we're here."

He stretched, on the seat.

"This is Antigonish?"

"So it would seem."

The town glimmered in the darkness like any other town. We couldn't make out the city hall on Main Street, or St. Martha's Hospital, or the campus of St. Francis Xavier University. Just the rooftops, the elevated silhouettes of a few buildings, and a good hundred dim lights beneath a pale grey sky. Menaud took out his notebook and made a cross in it.

"The Cabot Trail, check."

"You slept all the way, Menaud."

I took a mouthful of beer, which by then was as fresh as piss in an iron pail.

"Which means what?"

"That technically, you didn't see the Cabot Trail."

"I've just done three hundred miles on it."

I let that go. The week before, we'd passed the site of one of the oldest abandoned mines in eastern Canada. I'd never worked in a mine, but my father was a miner, and already in 1969 I'd seen in his eyes, on his clothes, and in his body, his bent back and his stiff neck, enough of mines to do me for a lifetime. Chopping down trees wasn't any less hard, but at least you were outside. I'd taken advantage of the fact that Menaud was sleeping to drive right past. When he woke up, he'd said:

"Are we getting near the mine?"

"The mine? We passed it an hour ago. You were sleeping like a log. Anyway, that would have put us behind schedule."

"We're going back."

"What?"

"We're going back."

"I just told you we passed it an hour ago."

"We're going back."

"For God's sake, Menaud. We'll get there in the dark."

"We're going back."

There was no point trying to reason with him. We went back. The mine was like a series of crude stairways carved into a meteorite crater. He looked at it for about ten seconds before making a cross in his notebook. That's how Menaud travelled.

We found ourselves a hotel, but I didn't sleep for long. In the morning we visited the town on foot. After, we stopped to eat. In all my life, I've never seen anything so disgusting as Menaud's breakfasts. He put ketchup on his eggs and mustard on his toast. He poured syrup on his bacon, and when he found an accommodating waitress, he added a fried onion on top of all that.

I was going to leave for Cape Breton in the afternoon, aiming for the other side of the island, to visit Louisbourg. In '61, archaeologists, historians and architects had begun the reconstruction of an old French fortress that had been destroyed by the English in 1759. I really wanted to see that, but Menaud didn't want to have anything to do with it. He'd decided to stay in Antigonish while I was there. I'd have to come back and pick him up, and return to Quebec via New Brunswick. It wouldn't be a big detour to go back through Antigonish, unless Menaud ended up drunk in some ugly duckling's sheets, and made me search for him all over town. I'd have preferred to keep him with me.

"You're sure you don't want to come?"

"Forget it. No way I'm going another hundred miles just to see some pencil pushers digging a town out of the mud."

He always talked that way. I worked to pay for my education, he worked because beer doesn't come out of the water tap. Travelling through time and space both was just a bit too much for him. That was about it.

"You shouldn't talk that way, Menaud. Seems to me you were born in the mud too, like tadpoles or couch grass, and you crawled up to your parents' farm. Your mother adopted you because she thought you looked pathetic with your little girl's legs and your monkey's ears. She was never very particular about men in any case."

I know plenty of people who would have punched me in the face for less than that, but not Menaud. He liked playing the tough guy, he liked to say he'd been in prison, and he was the only man I'd ever met who you could flatter by saying his father had been a thief and his mother a whore.

He gave me a big smile with his rotten teeth.

"Yeah, maybe that's what happened."

I took off on my own. I wasn't afraid. In those days people told all kinds of stories about drivers picking up white-faced hitchhikers who vanished without a trace right in the middle of a trip. No one had ever told me about a woman in a red coat haunting the Cabot Trail, and anyway mine wasn't even thumbing a ride. She was just there, looking out over the high seas with her dry hair, as if our nights were her days, as if she saw, in the midst of the storm, an enormous sun shining over the strait. Of course, I know I didn't see a ghost on the road that night. I may be old now, but I'm not crazy. Except it's remained a mystery to me, not knowing who put that woman in my head, who'd given her that silhouette and that face that I'd never seen anywhere. There's something unknowable in all that, like how you can never really tell if it's the water, the wind, or the salt adrift in the wind that carves animal shapes and women's faces out of the fjords.

The Montagnais who cut wood with the rest of us in the camp, I always asked him to tell me what the Indians called the places we went. One day when we were really far north, I asked him the name of the lake where we'd stopped for lunch. He shrugged his shoulders.

"You don't know?"

"It's not that. Your lake has no name."

"What do you mean, no name?"

"No one ever comes here."

Unless they had a good reason, the Indians never strayed from their traditional portages and their navigable waterways, and they felt no need to give names to places they never visited. It was a European obsession to go everywhere and it became an American obsession to build roads that led nowhere. Those roads, Menaud and I, we'd done at least half of them. We couldn't count them in those days, we couldn't know where they would lead. America was a kind of big asphalt map traced right onto the land, a continent to rediscover. I'm sure they're all labelled now, those roads, mapped so you can follow them with a finger on your GPS. My son-in-law has even bought a car that talks. It's always telling him he's taken the wrong road, and I'll be damned if I'll ever let a machine speak to me like that.

After 1971 I never heard from Menaud, I didn't know if he was alive or dead, and I decided that one morning he must have gone back to the mud at the fort of Louisbourg, or where he came from. We'd travelled together for a long time, he and I, and we'd probably still be travelling together if I hadn't met Louise during my last year at university. We'd never much called each other my beauty or my love, nor later my wife or my husband, but one day she said to me, "If you like, we could get married." It's not a great love story, certainly, but it's ours. I'd never thought about marriage before, but I said yes right away, and later I realized that was exactly what I wanted. We had four daughters more beautiful than their mother and more intelligent than me. They're big now, but they can't leave hold of their mother, whom they telephone three times a day. They have the whole world at their feet, and you'd think they were afraid of everything. It's something I can't understand.

Louise is a doctor, and I was a forestry engineer. She's spent her life taking care of people, and I've spent mine taking down trees. That's the way it is. In a few months, she'll be retiring too. And we'll travel. We've travelled already, but not much in recent years. Louise likes it a lot, but not me. They always hold us by the hand on those tours, and it seems to me that you can't really travel bundled up with other little oldsters in a bus, with guides who explain everything you see through the window like you're all six-year-old children. I'd like to show her the ground we covered, Menaud and I, back then.

Meanwhile I garden, I read, and I do errands. About four o'clock I go out to buy what we need for the night's meal and the next day's lunch. They've built a big supermarket right next to Canadian Tire, on the other side of the overpass. You have to turn right for the groceries and left for the highway. I often turn left. Louise knows it, just as she knows that I always come back in the evening with the supper.

Cryptozoology

LATE JUNE.

Half asleep, Jim hears the rain falling non-stop onto the truck, the two woodsheds, and the piles of wood waiting to be dried, cut, split. He imagines the rivulets streaming down the little dirt path winding its way to the road for kilometres through angiosperms and gymnosperms, the great cavalcade of all the species present at that latitude, spared by the forestry company because it wasn't worth their time to clear the concave tongue of land stretching from their camp to the road between two mountains. Half asleep, Jim knows his land and knows that the rain is irrigating the sugar maples, the cherry trees, the paper birch, the black ash, the trembling aspen, the red oak, the linden trees, two white pines as tall as the CN Tower, the rotten trunk of an American elm, centenarian three times over, that had to be cut down because it was sick with bark beetles, the balsam fir, the white spruce and black spruce, the Canadian thuja, the red-fruited sumac from which Doris, in the summer, makes a kind of acid lemonade, and the mountain ash with their big orange fruits that drive the birds crazy. Jim hears a great mad wind that's blowing through the trees and whistling between the walls and under the outhouse roof.

Half asleep, he's on the same plane as the other forest creatures, waiting for the storm to calm where they lie on their beds of branches, leaves, and moss, less comfortable than his own. Though he's seen the bad weather heal itself a thousand times, part of him thinks the squall will last forever.

Half asleep, Jim tells himself that the rain will stop and that, as always after a storm, the animals will come out of their shelters in search of sun. As the first light shines through, the partridges let their chicks frolic out in the open on the gravel paths, and the rabbits swarm like insects along the roads, veering off very late, sometimes too late, when they hear tires crunching on the gravel. It's during this brightening that he's seen the rarest animals. The black bear on the woodcutters' camp road. The moose that crossed the Joe Roth River while he was teasing trout massed in a shadowed bowl, with great arcing casts. The lynx by the lake, crouched in grasses, under branches. Half asleep, Jim can tell by the weight and smell of the air that the rain won't be stopping for a while and that he must summon the patience of the other animals, those that hunt, those that answer to the periods of the moon and only come out at night.

He gets up and puts water on the stove to heat in an old iron kettle, and goes out on the porch to gather logs and birch bark from the wood box. The air is cool, humid inside and out, and the cabin floor is as cold as a steel spoon before you dip it into the soup. His father stirs in his bed and opens his eyes. The water begins to rumble in the kettle. His father emits a sigh that becomes a rattle, then a coughing fit, and asks:

"What's new?"

"Not much, pa. You?"

His father sits up in bed.

"We wanted to go fishing with Luce. We took the rods and the tackle, then Luce waited in the boat while we loaded the cooler on, then the worms. She was wearing your mother's hat, with a really nice army jacket."

Jim lights the balled up newspaper he'd thrust into the stove under the crossed logs.

"Did you catch anything good?"

"No. At the last minute Réjean arrived and said he didn't want her to go with us. So we never went."

"And then?"

"Then nothing. I was in the dark. There was lightning and thunder and it was raining just like now. Maybe I wasn't asleep any more, just turning over and over in bed."

He clears his throat.

"Did you see your animal again?"

The day before, they'd gone to Armand Guay's at Lac de la Belette. They'd brought him beer from down below. When they arrived, Armand handed a bottle to his father, and asked Jimmy if he wanted to go fishing. Jimmy knew it was a way of getting him out of the way so as to get drunk with his father in peace, but they'd been in town for a week and Jim was dying to put his line in the water. He said yes, and Armand's dog followed him to the dock and jumped in the boat without his having to say a word. He started the motor with three good pulls on the cord, and headed north towards the islands that block access to the bay. Lac de la Belette is full of pools and tributaries, and he fished for a long time with Sunny seated in the stern. Jim got a bit scared when it became dark, but right then there was an electric sizzle in the air. Armand had started the generator, and the lights over the boathouse burned bright like a beacon set into the mountain.

In the cabin, Armand and his father were drunk. Murielle, Armand's wife, was also drunk, but less than Réjean and Luce, who had arrived in the meantime. The adults were playing cribbage, drinking, shouting, and talking sex under their breath, thinking Jim wouldn't understand. Jim made himself a grilled cheese sandwich. He prepared coffees with some local brandy and whipped cream for the women, then when he was tired of it all, lay down on the couch behind the table with Sunny alongside him. About three in the morning, his father woke him and said, "We're off."

Jim always drove through the bush when his father was drunk. He helped his father climb into the truck and wended his way slowly along the forestry company's road. His father was snoring beside him when it happened, just before the pitted incline that always made him nervous, and that the truckers called Gear Hill, full of ruts where they often broke their transmissions. An animal was walking far in front of the truck, crossing the road diagonally. He was never able to say what it was. Not a bear or a moose. It was too big for a fox and too high on its legs to be a lynx. His father had woken up, and he wasn't sure either. In the glare of the headlights, its fur looked tawny or white. Almost silvery.

In bed, his father turns to the wall and stifles a cough.

"Yes," says Jim, "I saw it again."

"Was it your cat?"

"No."

In his sleep, Jim went over the drive on Gear Hill, slowed then sped up, turned on his high beams and hit the horn, trying to immobilize the animal. He didn't see it any better than the day before, but he replayed it enough times to understand it better.

"It was a wolf, Pa."

"You're sure?"

"Pretty sure."

"Could've been worse."

They always talk that way, as if their dreams weren't dreams at all, as if they each lived the night, then the day, like two lives, one inside the other, of which one, but never the same one, sometimes seems stranger than the other. The kettle begins to whistle. Jim goes to the counter, throws three spoons of coffee into the bottom of the pot, and pours in water. He lowers the piston very slowly, millimetre by millimetre. The cottage smells good of burnt wood and steaming coffee.

"I made you coffee. Want Aspirin too?"

"Please."

He gives him four without thinking twice, and brings him a glass of water. Back from Armand's the night before, his father went to the outhouse while Jimmy turned on the gas and opened the cottage, making his way through the darkness with the help of his flashlight's dim beam. His father came out of the toilet reeling, his pants down to his ankles, and his penis bobbing left and right in the night air. Climbing the steps to go into the house, he stumbled over the bear board. Jim had to wrench the plank full of nails off the sole of his boot, support him as far as the bed, help him to get undressed, and toss his underclothes and underpants stained with piss, blood, and shit into a garbage bag.

Ordinarily, Jim didn't go to a lot of trouble for his father the morning after a night of drinking, but yesterday, at Lac de la Belette, just before his father woke him up, Jim saw him through his half-closed eyelids over the furred neck of the dog that was lying on top of him, and he was kissing Luce. They embraced for a long time, then Luce murmured something in his ear and they separated. Jim didn't know where the others were. Fallen in combat, probably. Jim may be barely thirteen years old, but he's old enough to know how a man feels, having enjoyed the kisses of a drunken woman the night before, which she would not have accorded him were she sober.

"If your head doesn't ache too much later, we could maybe get dressed and go fishing. Should be good after the rain."

"We could. If the weather gets a bit better. Let me drink my coffee and eat something first. You want eggs?"

The man from whom his father had bought the cabin eight years earlier did not fish, and only went there for the big hunt in autumn and to get drunk in winter on his skidoo. The house was too far from the main road for there to be visitors. The lake, their lake, which like a horseshoe embraced the chalet on its peninsula, had practically not been fished for ten years. That ought to have made it a paradise for fish breeding, but it's not what happened. Left in peace, the trout had prospered and increased in size in the lake, before growing scarce beneath its placid surface.

At a certain point, they'd begun to cannibalize each other.

You need patience to fish on the lake. Jim and his father pull in barely twenty trout a year, but they're all as big around as a forearm, with the protruding brow of a freshwater salmon. On the skin of their backs, stippled with red, blue and black dots and the colour of old steel, dark meshing runs between the head and tail, around a dorsal fin as stiff in the cold water as that of a shark. Their bites can't be compared with the electric tugs little stream trout give to the line. At first it's as if a diver hidden in the lake has rolled the line around his fist before giving it a good yank. Then, once well hooked, they heave with all their strength towards the bottom, running the line and bending the rod until its joints start to creak. At the last moment, they'll sometimes rise and slam against the side of the boat, snapping the hook or ripping it from their mouths with a hard, sharp jolt. At the end of May, just after the lakes have crested, when you dip your hand in the icy water to rinse off the blood and silt, you'd think the lake was sinking its teeth into your flesh like a creature that's more rapacious still.

★

Early November.

You've gotta have lots of time to waste, Doris said, to run after a hare in the deep woods in the middle of November, but that's exactly what Jim is doing, leaning forward to try and see the hare's silhouette under the bell-shaped firs, their branches weighed down by the heavy snow, his arm muscles stiff from holding the rifle, his clothes soaked with sweat and the water dripping from firs and spruce. He's climbing towards the road, his lungs on fire, he hears his own steps cracking dead branches under the snow, his own breath, and the brook water down in the coulee burbling away under a thin film of ice.

He and Doris had seen the hare cross their path as they were following the trap line on their four-wheeler, a big Yamaha Grizzly. They got down from the Grizzly to follow it. The hare was very small, but searching for it they flushed another one, a beautiful fat hare, well primed for whatever winter might send its way. Jim kept his eyes on it for a while, where it was moving about in the midst of a small stand of birches that had lost their last leaves two weeks earlier, but it kept stopping with its back turned, in a position that gave you nothing to shoot at. Jim would have liked nothing more than to cram lead up its backside as far as its ears. Doris gave up the chase pretty fast.

"Go on and follow it," she said. "I'm going back for the four-wheeler. I'll be there when you come out onto the road."

She embraced him the way she always did, whether he was on his way to the outhouse or going to the dock for water, without holding back, as if he were off to the war or leaving forever.

The woods are so dark that he's dazzled when he comes out onto the road. He adjusts his eyes to the light, looks about, and sees, to the right, fifteen metres ahead, the hare, a bit set back under the branches beside the path, still facing away. He begins to move forward quietly, taking long steps like a tight-rope walker so as not to frighten it. He hears Doris coming up behind him in the Grizzly, and he knows the hare is going to bolt in a few seconds. It turns its head towards him. Jim shoulders the gun, aiming a bit to the side, and fires. The rifle goes hot in his hands. The hare shudders and falls in the road, its body shaken by small convulsions. Doris arrives. Jim takes a few steps towards the hare, and suddenly stops.

A dozen metres in front of him, in a spot where the trail becomes less well defined, half hemmed in by the willows, an animal that's a lot bigger than a hare is sitting, its back to him, surrounded by trees. Jim's heart is pounding. Behind his shoulder he signs to Doris in the Grizzly to stop. He ejects the empty cartridge from his gun, shoves it into his vest pocket, then rummages underneath in the pocket of his shirt. His gun is a 12-gauge Remington 870, with a short barrel for hunting deer. Jim uses it for hares and partridge, because it's easy to handle in the thick bush where he's always hunting. The chokeless barrel produces a nice pattern of scattered shot that's good for bringing down partridges in flight and allows him to cut off the head of his prey on the ground without damaging the rest of the carcass. The barrel can shoot deer slugs, and before he leaves on a hunt his father always gives him two or three, well separated from the dozens of cartridges loose in his pants pocket and jacket. It's his insurance policy in case he runs into wolves, a bear, or an ill-tempered moose.

He loads a slug into the gun and closes it very gently while pushing the pump forward. Describing a wide arc in the road, he circles the animal until he finds himself face-on to it, always alert for a movement, his breath shallow. It's a big cat, a yellow-brown feline with big ears, black at the ends, still not moving as it sees Jim approaching with the gun aimed at its head. Jim passes in front of a still snow-covered fir, and then he understands. The cat's head is a bit bent, as if it's pondering, its eyes fixed on the ground. Against the white background you can see a black line running from the cat's head to the trunk of an arched black ash sapling. It's a lynx caught in a snare. Jim sees Doris approaching, and smiling broadly.

"I'm pretty lucky to have a white knight protecting me from dead lynxes."

"Don't give me a hard time, Doris."

"No, no."

Side by side they walk to the lynx, which must have been caught while hugging the ground, chasing a hare. Kneeling in front of it, Jim sees its pink tongue hanging out, and its yellow gaze, befogged, like milky tea or the pastis his father drinks in summer after he's poured in a few drops of water.

"It's not even a good time for lynx. I keep telling Bernard not to make his fox snares too big."

"Are we on Bernard's territory?"

Bernard is another trapper who shares territory with Doris and her husband, the trapper Jacques Plante.

Jim frowns. Doris blushes.

"Yes. I took this path because I know there are always lots of birds and hares."

"I told you I didn't want to make you take detours during your runs."

"And I'm telling you that I don't see you that often, that I like hunting with you, and I'll always have time to take care of them on my own, my runs and my traps."

They smile at each other.

Afterwards they pick up the hare, free the lynx, load it onto the front bumper of the four-wheeler, and hurry to drop it off with Bernard so as to get back before nightfall. On the hills, this time of the year, darkness drops down like a curtain, between two blinks of an eye.

Doris lets him drive, and climbs up behind him. Before heading off, he raises himself up to properly check out, from that angle, the dead lynx held in place by two elastic straps. Doris says, behind his back:

"A beautiful cat, eh?"

"Yes."

"But not *your* cat."

"No."

She kisses him on the cheek, wraps her arms around him, and says:

"He couldn't be far."

In autumn, during the moose hunt, Jim wasn't allowed to shoot with his 12 gauge or his father's .410 bore. Hunters in ambush didn't want to have guns going off around them left and right.

For partridges, his father had bought him a lead shot break-action rifle with a little telescope. It could bring down a bird from quite close range, as long as you avoided the wing's protection and aimed for the head or the base of the neck. Flushing the birds was a totally different kind of hunting from taking them down in flight. You had to spot the partridges from a distance, huddled together and camouflaged in the woods, approach without spooking them, and make a good shot. In the woods along the road you killed ruffed grouse, whose male was like a red-brown cock very high on its legs. Amid the spruce and the fir you killed Canada grouse, whose male did not sport a ruff, but whose breast and black head were spotted with white, and whose eyes were topped by thick red wattles. The females of the two species had the same cryptic grey-brown plumage, and it was almost impossible to distinguish them before cutting open their breasts with a knife. The ruffed grouse had the white, delicate flesh of a cockerel, whereas the flesh of the Canada grouse was a violet-red that resembled very lean beef when cooked, and tasted strongly of fir foliage and juniper.

Often, the bird perched on a branch or curled on the ground amid the leaves and moss didn't die right away. It went into convulsions, performing a backlit St. Vitus's dance, soul-stricken against the sun, amid airborne feathers wrenched from its own plumage. His father had showed him what to do in such a case. You had to seize the flapping bird in a swift lunge, immobilize it, then crush its trachea between your thumb and index finger. If you put your hand on its breast at the same time, you could feel the bird's heart quake beneath the skin and feathers, race, panicked, then finally pound out three or four heavy dull pulsations before stopping dead. His father said, "That's what it is to kill something, Jim. You kill better when you've understood that. If you can't do it, you shouldn't hunt. You shouldn't shoot anything."

Jim had done it once that day. He'd had his stomach turned upside down, and for a whole season he'd stopped shooting at the partridges he'd flushed, so he wouldn't have to do it again.

Then he got over the horror.

It became a terrible, beautiful thing that came back every autumn, the first bird brought down whose tiny heart he smothered between his hands. Every time, he placed his hand on the bird's body and matched his own breath to the pitch of the throbbing muscle. When the drumming stopped at last, he opened his eyes on the dead bird and discovered to his surprise that his own heart had not missed a single beat.

*

They always called him Jacques Plante the trapper to distinguish him from Jacques Plante the goalie. He's the one who'd first talked to him about the cat.

The year after the accident, Jim had spent almost all summer in the woods. His father left him with Doris and Jacques when he went down to the city. That summer, a doctor from Chicoutimi had set up a trailer nearby to fish on the surrounding lakes in a canoe. He'd probably intended to hunt moose there in the autumn. Doris and Jacques weren't crazy about that, but they'd decided to be gracious with Doctor Duguay, as they were with everyone. The doctor had a dog, Spencer, a good-looking boxer with cropped ears, who didn't seem quite at home in the middle of the thinned out forest.

Doris and Jacques also had an old dog that was to die the following year. His name was Boss. He'd been Jim's best friend since he was born, and was perfectly at ease in the woods. He was a very big dog, a cross between a German Shepherd and a malamute. The doctor had come to visit them one night when it was the time for a fire, and the trappers' camp was full of people. He'd stayed there, standing, had refused to sit and take a beer, and had advised them to tie Boss up during the day. "That would be safer," he'd said, "Because Spencer is a dominant male."

Doris and Jacques had consented. He'd left quietly, heading back to his trailer. The trappers never tied Boss up, and one fine day the big wolf dog had come out of the woods at a trot, around dusk. Jim's father was there. They were all sitting around the picnic table, eating corn and hot dogs. Boss was holding Spencer in his mouth, by the neck. The boxer was unrecognizable. Boss deposited the corpse at their feet, as if it were a huge hare, all disjointed.

Jacques tied Boss to a post and they left, with his father, for the doctor's trailer. On foot. As if there would have been something sacrilegious in transporting the dog by truck or in a four-wheel drive. His father and Jacques walked in single file along the path, taking turns with Spencer, whom they carried like an armful of logs. Doctor Duguay was all alone in his trailer, playing solitaire by the light of a gas lamp. He wasn't hysterical or angry or sad. He took Spencer from the trapper's arms and asked:

"What happened?"

"I don't know, doctor. I found him like that while checking my snares."

"Your dog?"

"Oh, he was tied up, doctor. And Boss would never have been able to do anything like that."

"What then? A bear? Wolves?"

"Oh, he would have defended himself against a bear better than that. And wolves don't go for the throat that way. Excuse the expression, doctor, but they would have torn him to pieces. But I'll tell you what could have done it. You can believe it or not, it's all the same to me. A long time ago they sometimes killed really bad cats around here."

"Lynxes?"

"A lot bigger than a lynx. I'm talking about something about as big as a tiger, that could jump from over there to this tree here without even having to take a run at it. An animal that would make a meal of just about anything. From a rabbit to a moose."

"So there's a big cat in the hills?"

"Like I said doctor, you don't have to believe me. I can only tell you what I know. There's been no big cat killed around here for a hundred years, but I know some fellows who are in the woods all the time like me, who say it's still there."

The doctor was thoughtful for a moment. Jim's father took the opportunity to add:

"If it turns out that your dog disturbed this cat while he was on a scent. You can't know what one, that of an animal maybe, but maybe yours, or my son's."

"If that's what happened," said Jacques, continuing the train of thought, "then maybe Spencer saved Jim's life."

The doctor decided to bury Spencer right away behind the trailer. He brought out some scotch that the three men guzzled from the bottle while digging the hole, and he gave Jim a Saguenay Dry. By the time they headed back it was dark and they were drunk and it was Jim who lit the way with his flashlight. When his father and Jacques had gone a good distance from the trailer, his father said:

"That was some lie."

In the trappers' cabin, a bit later, Jim went up to Jacques and asked:

"Trapper, did it ever exist, that creature you were talking about before?"

"What creature?"

"The big cat."

The trapper pointed to the shelf about two feet from the ground running around the cabin's four walls. On that shelf there were the whitened skulls of dozens of animals, in decreasing size. It began with two big bear heads and five wolf heads, going down to the many tiny heads of martens and mink, of groundhogs and squirrels. Between them there were the heads of coyotes, of lynx, of foxes, of fishers, of porcupines, and even a wolverine. All that was missing was a moose, but a large set of antlers was attached to a horizontal beam and rose up over their heads, casting frightening shadows onto the ceiling.

"I'm going to tell you something, Jim. If it's not on the shelf, it doesn't exist."

"Yes, but Jacques, there's no human head on the shelf, and they exist."

The old man smiled and brought his old hands down, like an eagle's talons, onto his head.

"If you're going to be a smarty pants, yours'll be up there next."

The doctor decided to move, and to set up his trailer a little less deep into the Controlled Harvesting Zone, where all the species were tracked. Still, he came to see us two or three times over the following weeks and he'd made his own inquiries. There really had been, he said, a big cat in the mountains. A ferocious animal, two metres in length, and capable of mighty leaps. Perhaps it was still there, yes, it was entirely possible, and that would explain everything. Doctor Duguay liked to sprinkle his sentences with Latin phrases, and from his grand pronouncements Jim had retained one term that echoed in his head ever after.

Felis concolor couguar.

★

Late January.

The men are gathered around the broken trap, far enough away not to interfere with the prints in the snow that start in a small coniferous wood on the other side of the small valley where they've left their skidoos, cross the snow-covered land, sweep around the shattered cage, and plunge even deeper into the bush. Jim had been able to follow them for thirty or so metres before losing them for good between two big balsams, whose warmth had made soft holes in the snow.

"You say that nobody's seen that bugger since the 1940s?" asks Bernard.

"1938," says Jim. "They killed it at the Maine border."

"And they've come back?"

"Maybe they never left. Hard to know."

Bernard looks at Jacques Plante the trapper.

"And you believe that?"

"It's not a matter of believing or not believing. There are some biologists from the University of Montreal who put out some bait. About fifty miles that way. They must know what they're doing."

Jacques Plante the trapper, on his snowshoes, bends over the two paw prints, big as saucers. Between the prints there are lines you'd say were whipped into the snow with sticks. Jacques clears his throat, sends a large gob of spit flying forwards, and looks in turn at Bernard, his brother-in-law Roland, and Jim.

"That sure looks like your cat. To make lines like that in the snow, you need a big tail."

Doris, sitting against a birch trunk a few steps behind them, says:

"It could have been a wolf."

"Yeah, but they don't hang out around here this time of the year. And that's not a wolf I saw."

Very early that year, November burst winter wide open to let in the wind from the northwest, and a little dry cold that bit into your cheeks and chilled your blood. Everyone is dressed in thick fur jackets or parkas. Doris and Jim are also wearing scarves over their lined hoods, to protect their faces. The sun is an opalescent smudge in a white sky that glints on the dark glasses of Bernard and his brother-in-law. The trapper asks:

"Find any hairs?"

"Nope."

"And the pictures, Jim?"

"The pictures? Not great."

Jim's holding a digital camera in his hands that's very practical because you don't need film and you can see your photos on it right away. But those machines don't like it when it's really cold. The screen keeps flashing the message, "Battery error." Jim has to turn the camera off and heat it up in the inside pocket of his coat before turning it on again. Twice already he's scrutinized the least blurry of the three shots Bernard took, on a screen not much larger than a postage stamp. He saw black lines and blotches in streaks on a white background, he recognized the leafless trees and the conifers pushing up from the thick layer of snow on the ground. Beyond, behind a scrawny spruce and the thick trunks of two birches, there was an indistinct patch of fairly dark beige. Peering at it, squinting his eyes before the sun and the gleam of the sun on the snow, he saw the muscled torso of an animal take shape, with two powerful legs and a tail thrust into the air like an apostrophe. He followed the shape frontwards until he saw the head almost totally hidden by a tree trunk, and then part of the face, the curving arch of an eyebrow, the erect tip of an ear, the muzzle with a black spot on its surface, and the vague silhouette of a small creature thrust into its mouth like a gag. The camera freezes again, and now Jim can no longer reconstitute the image with so many details. Every time he turns on the camera the picture seems softer, as if someone had wanted to take a photo through a window just to capture his own reflection in the glass.

Bernard's skidoo had broken down earlier in the day, while he was making the round of his traps with Roland. As he had his snowshoes and he knew he was very near two traps, he sent his brother-in-law back to the camp for spare parts and tools. They were on a large expanse of level ground, and Bernard began to advance, hearing no sound but the crunching of his snowshoes in the snow, the buzz of the other departing skidoo, and from time to time the cry of a squirrel. After walking for ten minutes he entered the dark woods, and stopped short on hearing a loud commotion. He advanced slowly, making no noise. He saw a large beast tearing apart his trap to reach the animal trapped inside. He was never able to say if it was a marten or a mink, because the huge creature fled, bearing it off between its jaws. Bernard had time to take a few photos before it was out of sight. He was panting, his heart was pounding, and by the time he got back to the skidoo he was close to blacking out. He took his portable radio and called Jim's father on their usual frequency, "I think I've just seen Jim's cat," he said.

Afterwards, he gave them his coordinates with the GPS. Jim and his father dressed rapidly, and his father filled the skidoo's gas tank while Jim called Jacques Plante the trapper and Doris on the radio.

Now they're all there, studying a photo that reveals nothing, and tracks that will have largely disappeared by the next day, when the Wildlife Service agent arrives. Jim should be disappointed but he isn't, not that much. He and his father take off on their skidoo and criss-cross through the underbrush until darkness falls, taking turns at the controls and peering as far as they can through the branches and trees. His father talks always of his cat in the singular, and Jim very much likes that.

"You'll see, we'll find it," he says. "One fine day it'll pop out right in front of us."

Of course, if there are still cougars around, it's logical that there would be several, but Jim also likes to think of it as a lone animal, immortal, like the Yeti or the Loch Ness Monster, a creature that hides for the pleasure of being tracked, and shows itself from time to time to revive its own legend.

In these valleys where it sometimes snowed non-stop for days at a time, and where violent thaws and freezes succeeded each other with no sequence or logic, winter was more than a season, it was a landscape superimposed on another, where you had to orient yourself according to rare, unvarying signs in the snow and the intense cold.

Gaétan Fournier, a friend of Jim's father, had his cabin in the bottom of a valley. There the accumulation of snow was so great that one year, at Christmas, Gaétan, his wife, his daughters and his sons-in-law, had to dig out the cabin with shovels from eleven o'clock in the morning until dusk. He'd stopped in the middle of nowhere on immaculate terrain, had got down from his skidoo and begun to take his snowshoes and round point shovel out of the sleigh. One of his sons-in-law had said:

"What are you doing, sir? Seems to me that the camp is still quite a ways."

Gaétan had replied:

"The camp is under my feet."

They'd shovelled as far as the cottage, lit a fire for the women with the wood they'd brought with them, and then shovelled some more until they'd reached the woodshed. They'd taken out logs and made a great inferno in the snow, slathering the wood with old motor oil. The next day their camp and its surroundings formed a huge crater in the snow-covered valley.

The snow built up on spruce and fir, gathered in thick layers that the deep cold hardened onto their branches. As of mid-December, whole hectares of the forest were transformed into dolmens of white ice that blazed under the boreal sun, as dangerous for the eyes as a welder's flare. People came from the ends of the earth to meander through this lunar, monotone landscape.

When an outsider asked local people if they had a name for what they saw, they replied, "We call them ghosts."

★

Early May.

Half asleep, he's running on four legs, is conscious of the strength of his muscles in movement, and feels branches brushing against his fur. In great bounds he leaps the rushing water and dead trees that the forest throws up in his path. Half asleep, he hears his father, Doris, and Jacques Plante the trapper talking, seated around the table a few metres from his bed. He knows the beast is tracking something, he's breathing a heady smell through his nostrils, sees through his dilated pupils the prey's silhouette far in the distance, it stands out against the green of the trees, which he has never known so vivid. Half asleep, he swoops down on the prey and recognizes it. It is himself. The cougar is attacking him, and he is the subject of those fragments of conversation he's hearing from the far end of his dream.

"How long had it been since he'd had the sickness?"

"Four years."

There is silence. The beast buries its teeth in his throat and he tastes the salt warm blood that is loose in the creature's mouth.

"That mustn't have brought back good memories."

"Not really, no."

Two weeks earlier, Jim had come home alone from school, knowing that it had returned. It had been stalking him already for several days, like an evil shadow. He managed to open the door despite his trembling and the unruly beating of his heart.

His father, sitting at the counter, saw him come in, and leaped up.

"Jim, what's wrong?"

He wanted to talk, he wanted to cry out, but by that point it was already in total possession of his body. He was elsewhere. For a long moment his father looked on as his son's body was wracked by convulsions, arched back on the ground, the eyes rolled upwards, then he took him by the shoulders, turned him on his side, and began humming a lullaby while passing his hand over his sweat-dampened hair.

A few days after the crisis, he fell ill. The flu, which worsened over the period of a week. He wasn't eating, and had a consumptive's cough. His father took him to the doctor, who diagnosed a serious bronchitis and prescribed antibiotics and a great deal of rest. The next day, from his room in the city, Jim overheard his father talking on the ham radio he kept in the basement to communicate with people up north.

"He's not doing that well, Doris."

"Why don't you bring him up to the woods?"

"I can't, not before the weekend."

"We'll come and get him, then. Antibiotics are fine, but I've got two or three other things in mind."

Now he's in his bed at the cabin and it's night. His father had arrived a bit earlier, had sat down on the covers beside him and placed his hand on his chest. Behind them, Jacques Plante the trapper was seated at the table in front of a beer, eating pieces of cucumber. Doris was busy at the stove.

"Feeling better, boy?"

"Yes, papa."

"Yes, he's better. He's been eating well since this morning. But he sleeps, the little rascal. Now we're going to make you a mustard plaster and you're going to go beddy-bye. Same for you, old man, you're going to have a bowl of soup and some tourtière and you're going to bed. You look tired too."

Doris stirred up two teaspoons of dry mustard in a bowl, along with cornstarch and cold water. She spread the plaster over an old cloth that she applied to Jim's chest. It was hot and dizzying. After five minutes, she came to lift it off for a few seconds, and kissed him on the brow. After a half-hour, she took it away altogether.

Now Jim is dreaming and listening. He hears what they're all saying about him. He'd like to reassure them, to explain to them. He often has a dream with no up nor down, where the beast attacks him and devours him. It's a dream of carnivorousness and violence, but not of death. He does not expire while the cougar is annihilating his body, he fossilizes within the animal like a memory of flesh. In its belly he dreams himself into a child itself of dreams, the stillborn offspring of a legendary creature, and there's colour in the dream, and the sounds dogs make, dozing next to the stove.

"Jim's sleeping," says Doris.

*

Jim often fell asleep just so, and listened in snatches to adults talking close by. He rolled over in his bed, and an hour was gone. He missed whole swathes of conversation. At one point he realized that his father was lying in bed in front of him, and only Doris and Jacques Plante the trapper were up and about. Like diligent angels, they watched over their sleep, and put the cabin in order while talking quietly.

They picked up full ashtrays and set them on the counter with a little water in them before emptying them into the trash. Jacques Plante doused the last cigarettes in a bottle of beer. In one of the two big dented kettles that Jim went to fill every morning and night at the lake, they put water to boil on the large burner of the Vernois stove, whose high flames licked the metal almost to the bottom of the handle. Jacques Plante emptied the boiling water into the dish tub in the sink, and the shadows filled with long wreathes of vapour smelling of lemon soap. Doris washed and Jacques dried. Jim watched them intermittently, and always asked himself how Doris could keep her old hands in such hot water. Sometimes she herself misjudged her resistance and left one hand immersed for a bit too long, snatching it out with a quick yank, shaking it, and saying, "Goddam, that burns." When they had finished the plates and utensils, they put the other kettle to heat to make water for the glasses, which they left to soak until morning. They emptied the ashtrays and lined up all the empty bottles at the end of the counter. Afterwards, Jacques Plante cleaned the old plastic tablecloth with Windex and a rag. Half asleep, Jim sometimes heard Jacques Plante asking Doris if they'd forgotten something, but by the time Doris did the rounds and came to murmur words in Jim's ear about times to come and things that would get better, he was beyond hearing anything.

Jim slept. They had gone when he woke up in the middle of the night to lay a log on top of the embers in the stove, and he was sleeping when his father woke at sunrise, pulled on his jacket, and left the cabin in silence to see the day dawn rich in mist and dew.

In the Midst of the Spiders

HE TRAVELLED for weeks at a time, but it was always, whatever the city, the same airport, the same empty space, with its distant hubbub and jet-lagged travellers. He'd been killing time for twenty minutes, sipping a gin and tonic in the company of a red-faced fifty-year-old who was on the same flight. The man had told him his name, but he'd forgotten it. It wasn't like him to forget names. That was his job, handshakes and slaps on the back, significant winks. He could—he ought to—remember the name of any random mortal stumbled upon in an airport or a trade fair. When he happened to remember the first names of their wives and children, that was even better. He'd had a professor of public administration once who liked to say that memory was a muscle you could train. The professor knew by heart almost every country in the world and their capitals. That had impressed him. Now he'd memorized the names of several hundred clients, their birthdays, their addresses, and always two or three personal details. He remembered who was the record collector and who the fly fisherman, knew who was happily married or getting divorced, who had a pregnant daughter or a son in detox. He also remembered what everyone drank. People always feel close to someone who can order their liquor for them.

The trick was to never write anything down. He'd read somewhere that at the end of the nineteenth century, some people refused to have their pictures taken, fearing that the apparatus would steal their souls. It was probably a superstition, but this for him was a proven fact: you would never remember anything as long as you didn't get out of the habit of noting everything, everywhere, every chance you got.

Behind the airport's windowed walls, rain was pouring down. It was like being in a car wash. The planes, far off on the runway, were blurred, and perched on the asphalt, seemed hunched over like big wet crows. He took another sip. He could not for the life of him remember the damned name. He really must have been out of sorts. What's more, the guy was ready to eat out of his hand, to lend him his summer house for a month, and, if pressured a bit, to pay him ten cents a litre for the water that flowed from his tap. But that too was his line of work. To sell. He was very good at it, but that's not why he was here.

Michel arrived at about 4:30. That gave him about three quarters of an hour before catching his return flight. He took leave from his anonymous friend, left the bar, and sat at a table with Michel, a few metres away. He lit a cigarette. He'd stopped smoking ten years earlier, and had started again two weeks ago.

Michel had bad breath and wore a cheap suit that seemed to have spent the last week in a garbage bag. He disliked him intensely for that. He'd spent the entire flight going over everything that irritated him about Michel. His hygiene was suspect. Michel had lived in Montreal and spent his time trying to recall it, citing street names, restaurants, and bars to which everyone (he in any case) was totally indifferent. Michel carried around in his wallet dozens of photos of his three ugly daughters, and trotted them out on the slightest pretext. Michel was also a consummate ass-licker, who had concocted his own personal technique for flattering your ego in a way that was both understated and obscene. It was hard to go on in that vein, because in the end he was a good guy and everyone liked him fine. But he had to set all that aside. In the beginning he'd embarked on these meetings full of empathy and compassion, and it had almost done him in.

They talked about this and that for a few minutes, and three times he forestalled Michel's launching into his diorama of ugly daughters. A waiter brought another gin and tonic and a cup of hot water. Another reason to loathe Michel: he'd stopped drinking a long time ago. Tippling in an airport bar seemed even grimmer when he had to do it in the company of an abstemious imbecile who wandered the world with his pockets full of herbal teabags.

He short-circuited the conversation to the point where a deadening silence set in. He stared at Michel for a long time, pulling on his cigarette and blowing smoke over his head until he was sweating, squirming in his chair, and feeling strangled by the knot in his tie. Soon Michel could no longer endure his gaze, and he fixed his eyes on the water snaking its way down the windows, cleared his throat, and asked:

"Are you here for what I think?"

Without saying a word, without moving his head, with only his eyes, he confirmed, "Yes."

Michel gave a small, tight blow to the table with his fist.

"Does she know how much I brought in for her in the last year?"

"Almost 700,000 dollars. She had me and two accountants to remind her of that, but you know her: she's pretty well certain that without her no one would be able to see their nose in front of their face."

"Meanwhile, you're doing her dirty work."

"I'm chief executioner now. It's all I've been doing for months. Not one contract, not one sale."

Michel exploded:

"You want me to cry for you, maybe? I'm fifty-two years old, for God's sake. Fifty-two years old, a sick wife, and three daughters at university. What am I supposed to do, can you tell me that? What does that fucking cow think we're all going to do? That fucking fucking fucking cow..."

"Enough."

"Do you know everything I did for her, and her father before her?"

"You worked, Michel."

"We gave them our lives."

"And they gave you yours."

"We're even-steven, is that it?"

"That's not what I said."

Michel became sullen.

"How do you think the company's going to be able to function? That makes twelve who are gone."

"Ten."

"Who's going to keep things going?"

He stubbed out his cigarette.

"Between the two of us, I don't think she gives a damn. She must have awarded herself ten salary hikes in the last five years. She should be earning not far from half a million now, not counting bonuses. Her father's dead, her mother's convinced that everything's going just fine, and as long as our old contracts are bringing in money and she's chopping the payroll, the investors are happy. I think she's going to milk everyone like dairy cows and then shut things down."

"How many of us are there?"

"About four hundred, if you count manufacturing."

"What's she going to do afterwards?"

"I don't know. Get Botox shots. Adopt Chinese kids. That's about all she's been doing for five years."

"It's not right."

"I never said it was."

Michel shot him a dirty look.

"You're still going to clear us out one after the other, like your mistress's good dog."

He shrugged his shoulders.

"That doesn't seem to bother you very much."

"What do you want me to do?"

"Why don't you tell her to do her own dirty work?"

"Why didn't you say anything when the others were being let go? I'm no different from anyone else, Michel. The city's burning, and I'm praying that the fire will spare my house."

"Where are we heading, like that?"

"Nowhere."

Michel got up, tottered a bit, then found his feet.

He got up in turn, held out his hand, and said:

"No hard feelings?"

Michel stared at his hand vacantly, without taking it, more shaken than he wanted to show.

"You're the executioner now. And an executioner has no friends. Maybe she thinks we're worthless, but we'll pull things together, you'll see. We still have our clients, and we can sell them more than her garbage. But you? Have you thought that no one's going to want to help you when your turn comes?"

He sighed and looked at his watch.

"I'm going to have to catch my plane."

"Oh, excuse me. I don't want to detain you. Can you give her a message for me?"

"Of course, Michel."

"Tell her that I'd have liked her to have had some real children rather than the stupid little Chinese kids she's adopted, who she shows off everywhere to make it look like she has a heart. Tell her that I'd have liked her to have a real heart and real children and to have one of those children die right in front of her eyes. Will you tell her that?"

"I doubt it."

The seat was comfortable, but the third gin and tonic had been one too many. He felt groggy. His wife said he was drinking too much these days. She was wrong, he wasn't drinking more than before. He'd always liked to drink. These days, he found that beer had an acrid smell, cocktails tasted bland, and whiskies gave off an unbearable medicinal scent, but he swallowed them all the same. That's all that had changed.

He felt better now that it was over with Michel. He could sleep on the plane, and in a few hours he'd be home. He'd take a shower and drink a glass of wine. Wine was still good. A bit oily perhaps, but still good.

In the old house, his first wife had organized the gardens according to a tiresome geometry. The flowers and shrubs grew in tight rows, like in a greenhouse, they never mingled, you'd have thought it was the window of an industrious florist. The house was smaller now, the garden more confined, and his second wife had this virtue: she arranged the plants any old way. Perhaps there'd been some order in the beginning, but very quickly it had disappeared. He didn't know where the soil got its richness, but by mid-July the back yard looked like a jungle. The daturas became actual bushes, and every day produced dozens of big white flowers; the morning glories ran riot, climbing the length of the hedges and stippling the garden with hundreds of purple, blue, and violet blossoms; the roses showed no restraint, and as of the middle of June the Europeana and the two Prairie Stars produced dozens of flowers with delicate petals, and roses like an old lady's closed fists. There were also lilacs, an apple tree, tulips, and dozens of other species, perennials and annuals, climbers and crawlers. He liked to sit in the midst of all these exhalations, in a chaise longue, and sip Long Island Iced Tea while doing crossword puzzles. Between the stems of the flowers and the branches of the shrubs, black and yellow spiders tended large webs. He liked to watch them at work, see the good Lord's flies and beasties become trapped in them and be devoured. It was strange, if he'd come upon spiders that big in the house, he would have been shocked. In the garden, he was not at all put off. The spiders, sometimes, fell on him. He took them in his bare hands and dropped them delicately onto the leaves.

Someone was shaking his shoulder.

"They're announcing our flight."

It was his companion from earlier on, standing beside the table. He remembered, his name was André. He wondered if he'd been sleeping. He picked up his overcoat and his briefcase, and strode towards the gate.

Before leaving, Michel had said that his turn would come. Of course his turn would come. He'd never thought otherwise. Enormous spiders lived in his garden. Soon it would all be over, and he would make his home in their company, the yellow and the black.

América

THE FIRST mistake we made was to think we could bring off a coup like that after the Towers.

Big Lé's mother and sister had gone back to live two years in Costa Rica between 1999 and 2001. Lévis went to see them a lot during that time, including for almost three months in 2000, starting with the holidays, so as to make it through the millennium with his ass in the sun. That's when he met América and Luis, in the hotel restaurant his mother ran.

América was a waitress, and Luis was living in San Francisco. They were in love, but they couldn't find any way to bring her to the States. They never explained why. Maybe she had a record. She had no special skills to show the immigration people, and they couldn't get her a green card or a visa.

Big Lé went several times with me to the States to see if the border with Canada was full of holes. He told Luis that he could get América through and dump her in San Francisco, if he paid the price. They talked about it a lot when Big Lé was down there. That's the way it stood when Big Lé came back to Quebec.

Next summer Luis called him and asked if he'd agree to get América over the border for three thousand bucks. Lé should have said no, but he said yes. That's how our problems started.

Meanwhile twelve fucking ragheads hijacked some planes to plough them here, there, and everywhere, right in Uncle Sam's face.

Let's just say the borders got a little less leaky after that.

★

The second mistake was to bring along Bezeau.

The original plan was to leave Arvida by car, pick up América at Dorval, sleep in Montreal at Cindy's, my ex, then hit the road for Detroit the next day. We figured we could cross the border, then offer Luis, for a couple of thousand more, to bring his girlfriend all the way down to California. That made for a whole lot of driving, except between the time Luis called Big Lé to set things up, and when we were ready to head out, something else happened. The day after the Saint-Jean Baptiste party at Saint-Gédéon, Big Lé lost his licence when he hit a roadblock at nine in the morning where the road forked at Saint-Bruno. He'd swallowed some speed for dinner and some more at midnight. He wasn't drunk any more, but the amount of alcohol he'd ingested between that morning and the day before was beyond calculation. We needed another driver, or else I'd have to do it all myself.

When we brought him in on the deal, Bezeau was famous.

He'd just done two years for holding up the Walmart in Chicoutimi. That idiot had gone in with a 12-gauge shotgun and come out with the cash from the registers. Then the cops had got on his heels as he was leaving the parking lot. Don't ask me how, but he was able to outrun those guys for half an hour with his frigging old Topaz that did zero to 100 kilometres in about twelve minutes. They had to put down spike strips on the Boulevard des Saguenéens in front of the 247 convenience store. People saw him get out of the car and wait for the cops to come up to him, his arms in the air, giving them the finger.

We thought a guy like that must have steady nerves.

We were wrong.

In an old *Reader's Digest* at my father's they told the story of a man-eating tiger in India that had fed its whole litter with human flesh. A tiger that's tasted human flesh will be a man-eater for the rest of its life, because our meat is salted from the salt we eat.

It took fifty years to get rid of the five crazy tigers and their mother.

The oldest of the Bezeau brothers, he'd done more or less the same thing for his little brothers, but with cocaine.

Mike, the Bezeau who came with us, got into coke when he was twelve. He came from a tribe of thieves and bottom feeders who broke into cottages and garages for about a hundred miles around. And I don't think we're going to be rid of them before the end of the world.

A lot later we learned that he'd been totally out of his skull during his famous Walmart coup. He'd heard his brothers talking around the table about a dumb urban legend claiming that in all the Walmarts in the world there was a million dollars in hundred dollar bills stashed in a safe. Bezeau told everyone he was going to the convenience store, he picked up the one-shot 12-gauge that had belonged to his dead grandfather, and he took off for the Place du Royaume. It must have been 8:30 at night. Once there he stormed in, shouting at the top of his voice that he wanted the million. He bonked a cashier who called him a moron, he charged the cash desk, and, somewhat hysterical, he fired in the air, by some miracle not killing anyone. He realized that he'd left the rest of his cartridges in the car, and he fled the scene with about a hundred and sixty dollars in his pockets.

We'd already figured out that our criminal genius was mildly retarded. The day before we left, Big Lé gave him five hundred dollars out of the fifteen hundred he'd received as an advance. He told him to fill up on gas and to buy beer in cans, Molson

Ex or Labatt Blue, so they'd look like Coke or Pepsi, and to buy lots to eat so we wouldn't have to stop much on the way. When Bezeau came back, he'd bought us each a beef jerky, plain chips, vinegar chips, ketchup chips, and five grams of coke.

He apologized for having forgotten the gas and the beer, but he boasted about having got a good deal on the coke.

The worst of it was that crossing south through the parkland was like his very own Kryptonite. He'd only done it once, to go to prison, and by the time we got to the other end he was scared of his own shadow. Everything spooked him, he was afraid of being caught, and the last night, before crossing the border, he said:

"Anyway, if it's a fuck-up tomorrow, I'm spilling everything. I'm not going back inside just for your stupid plan."

There were two double beds in the room. América slept in one, Lévis and me in the other, and we'd installed Bezeau on the floor at the end of our bed like a little dog. I was the one who'd wanted to strangle him for the last two days, but finally it was Lévy who jumped him, with his two hundred and forty odd pounds. He threw himself at him on the floor and started hammering him with his fists on both sides of his head, shouting:

"Shut the fuck up, Bezeau. Shut your fucking mouth."

América, down on the ground, was weeping and wailing, *"Están locos, están completamente locos."*

Lévis got up, looked at her, and said:

"Cállate tú también. No jodas con la policía. No jodas con la coca. Quédate aquí y deja de llorar. Mañana estarás en Estados Unidos."

★

Our third mistake was not to have asked for enough money.

We left Montreal early, about seven in the morning. We took the 401 to the Ontario border, and drove until evening to Windsor, stopping to eat.

Before looking for a motel, we went for a walk along the Detroit River. At one point, there was a telescope. Big Lé put a whole quarter into the slot so América could see the other shore. She stayed there for a long time, gazing at Detroit. When Bezeau started getting restless, Lé said, "Just lay off, leave her alone."

As far as I know, she'd never seen the States so close.

I saw Lévis was getting nervous. We found a seedy-looking motel and checked in. Bezeau went to bed, and América came with the rest of us onto the terrace to take in the sun. Lévis told me there wasn't much money left out of the $1500. We phoned one of our buddies in Montreal, who knew a lot about the law, to ask his advice. The first thing he asked Lévis was:

"How much are you doing this for?"

"Three thousand."

"You guys really are babes in the woods."

Then he asked how we thought we were going to come back into the country with one passenger missing. Especially since Lévis had sponsored her for a visa.

"I thought I'd play dumb. At Canadian customs. I'll say I got taken and the girl took off with my cash."

"That's not bad. You won't be able to go back to the States for a good long time, but that's not bad. As long as Jay backs your story like he should. If I were you, I'd leave the other cokehead at the motel."

We looked at each other, Lé and me. The guy was right.

He went on:

"You're no big operator, Big Lé, but it's not worth losing your rep for a lousy three grand."

We agreed on a plan B. Lévis decided to call Luis to ask him for the rest of the three thousand bucks right away. It was Lévis's girlfriend in Jonquière who was checking to see if the money had been deposited in our account. We didn't have the

Internet on our cell phones back then. Luis was supposed to fork over the rest of the three thousand for us to get América across the border, and two thousand more once we were on the other side so we wouldn't haul her back with us. None of that money involved taking the girl all the way to California. We'd said, "Let them deal with it, Christ."

Lévis said:

"You take care of the girl. I'm calling Luis."

I said OK, but before hiding himself away around beside the reception desk, he added:

"Fuck it, I'm going to tell him that for two thousand more we can bring him América ourselves. We'll go down to San Francisco, just the two of us, with the girl. A total road trip. I'll drive without a licence, we'll be careful, and that's that."

"What do we do with halfwit?"

"Fucking halfwit, we throw him onto a bus, that's what."

*

The fourth mistake was to not get everything straight before leaving. When it came to the girl.

When América arrived at the airport, I said to myself, "Me, I'd go to bed with that girl." I was twenty-three years old, and she wasn't far off forty. Her face was a bit tired, especially the eyes, and she had a big explosion of black curly hair on her head. She was about so high, almost no breasts but a solid ass, and the most beautiful legs I ever saw on a woman. Above all she had a way of rolling her hips, a way of not being able to stop herself from rolling her hips, that made you choke on your saliva, let's say.

At first everything went fine with her in the car. Big Lé made her laugh, we pretended to understand her, and Lé's music rocked. But after a while, his mood changed. I didn't know why.

I knew that Bezeau, in the back, was getting on his nerves. That retard had brought along a whole kit just to turn coke into crack while we were on the road. He had a funny old spoon shaped like a ladle, a little medicine bottle full of baking soda, and a big bottle of distilled water. He put four parts of coke, one part of Cow Brand into the spoon, two or three drops of water, then he heated it from underneath with his lighter, while stinking up the whole car.

América said over and over, *"Están locos, están locos."* Where she came from, that was enough to get thrown in the hole for the rest of your days.

I wouldn't have wanted to be sitting beside him either, especially in her place. Smoking, it's not like snorting, it puts you to sleep sometimes. If you can call that sleep. Bezeau was having bad dreams right beside her. Rock dreams. He grabbed at his cock through his jeans, raging, murmurous, through his teeth:

"Here, my cunny. Here, my muffin. Here, my coochie."

We didn't quite know what he was talking about. Lévis would have put him up front with me, but the only time he'd tried to do so, after the dinner when he'd stayed in the car to smoke, he'd insisted he wanted to drive, and América had almost had a nervous breakdown.

I know that was more than enough to spoil a trip, but his mood had altered even before Bezeau had started freaking out.

I wanted to talk about it to Lévis that night, while he was having a smoke out on the terrace in front of the motel, but before I could open my mouth, he said:

"She's not his wife."

"Of course, if they were married, we wouldn't have to be doing this."

"No, what I mean is, she's not his woman at all. Maybe she was a vacation fuck in San José, maybe he owes her a favour, I don't know what, but she's not his woman and she'll never be his woman."

I agreed with him. Bezeau had told us all at least a dozen times that América had offered to suck him off the day before at Cindy's. It wasn't true, obviously, but you didn't need a sign as clear as that to see that América was nobody's woman. You could just tell, I don't know why.

I agreed with Lé, but I still asked him:

"Why are you saying that?"

"Because if I loved a woman and I wanted her to join me in the States, I wouldn't give the job to a couple of clowns like us."

He cleared his throat and spat a large gob onto the ground. He added:

"And if I loved a woman and some clown offered to set her down on my doorstep for two thousand dollars, I wouldn't say, 'Once you're over the border, do whatever you want with her.'"

Lévis got a text from his girlfriend at three in the morning. The money had arrived.

He told me to wake up América and to load up the car and wait for him outside. He woke Bezeau, who was sleeping like a log, and told him, "You're not coming with us to the border."

He gave him three hundred bucks to take a taxi to the bus station and a bus to the Saguenay in case we didn't come back. Bezeau kept shouting, "I can't even speak English, for Christ's sake!"

The voices got quieter, and Lévis came out by himself. We got in the car. He turned to América to say, *"Todo saldrá bien, guapa."* Then he looked at me and said, "Let's go."

The following Friday, Bezeau went to see Lévis at the bar where he was the doorman, to ask him when they were going to split the money.

"There's no more money. I gave it all to the girl. You, you got three hundred bucks worth of coke out of me, you didn't drive for two minutes, and you cost me a bus ticket. In my books I don't owe you a fucking cent."

Bezeau went off, cursing.

"Anyway, the next time you come up with a plan like that, don't call me."

"We won't call you, that's for sure."

*

Our fifth mistake was to go through Detroit.

If we were to do it again, I'd choose a little border crossing in Quebec with one sleepy guy and say, "We're going shopping in Plattsburgh." Back then we thought that passing through Detroit would give us a head start if Luis ever gave us the OK to push on all the way to California. In particular, we figured that the Ambassador Bridge had the largest volume of commercial traffic in the world, and that gave us a better chance to get through.

They had the traffic, yes, but they also had the means to manage it. Especially in the summer of 2002.

As we left the highway for the bridge early in the morning, the cars were flowing freely. But as soon as we hit the middle of the bridge, high above the river, we stopped moving entirely. We still had more than a kilometre to go, it was already hot, and my car's air conditioning wasn't working. We were completely soaked in sweat when we reached the customs booth on the American side. The guy looked at our passports.

"So you gentlemen are from Quebec and the lady here is from Costa Rica."

"Yes."

"Why are you coming to the United States?"

"To visit. She's never been here."

"All right. And why here?"

"I'm sorry?"

"Why travel this far to cross the state line?"

Lévis thought we were already fucked when the customs man saw the Costa Rica passport, but I think we were fucked right there. We had no answer for that. Lévis made one up on the spot. He gestured to the back with his head:

"Oh, she loves Detroit."

If we'd been less dumb, we'd have known that that was not an answer to give. Nobody likes Detroit, because Detroit is a shithouse.

He had us pull over and park, and escorted us inside. They took América aside and kept her for a long time. The two of us waited a good hour before a guy in a tie came to talk to us. My ears were ringing and my hands wouldn't stop sweating.

It's strange, because today I still remember what the guy said as if he was speaking French, even if that's impossible. Lévis tells me that it's the same for him.

The man said right off that we were welcome in the United States, but not the young woman who was with us. He said there was no formal accusation against us, but he thought he knew what we were up to. He said, "If you try it again, at any border crossing from the Rockies to the Adirondacks, today, tomorrow, or in six months, you really won't like what's going to happen to you afterwards."

We waited for an hour to get América back. She'd been crying. Lévis said to her, "*Lo siento, guapa.*" We went back on the 401, and I saw he was taking a detour to pass by the motel. I asked:

"Do we really have to pick up that fucking retard?"

"I'm not going back for Bezeau, I'm going back for the coke."

Bezeau had already left. Lévis went to see the Pakistani at the reception. He convinced him that he needed the keys to the room because he'd left something behind. That son of a bitch had hidden two grams between his mattress and the box spring.

"And the maid?"

"Does it look to you like the rooms here are cleaned very often?"

We headed straight back to Montreal, taking turns at the wheel, and sniffing coke off a key from time to time. América didn't say a word. Lévis never tried to find out what was behind it all. He didn't talk about what Luis had said either, but I think she knew. She didn't once ask to call him on the way back. Not once.

We arrived at Cindy's dead on our feet. I think we slept twelve hours straight. The next day we looked into how to get América to Costa Rica. She'd bought a calling card, and she spent her time talking to people in her country. She talked with Cindy, too. I don't know how they understood each other.

Lévis gave the girl almost all the cash. A thousand bucks. Back where she was going, that would be a lot of money.

The first night, we tied one on with some buddies at the Sainte-Élisabeth. The second night we left América with Cindy again and we both went to flame out the rest of the cash at the Solid Gold. We had three hundred dollars, but Lé wanted to save some money for gas, to get back to the Saguenay.

We drank rum and coke and beer and Jameson shooters. Lé paid me a session in the cubicle with the most beautiful dancer I'd seen so far. I don't know how much he gave her, but she stayed with me for at least six songs. I would have liked her to rub her pussy against me or shove her big tits in my face, but she didn't stop showing me her cunt. She had little lips bigger than the big ones, and she kept on playing with them and pulling on them as if they were her pride and joy or I don't know what.

In the end that kind of put me off, and I was embarrassed to look.

The last day, we got up late. América had gone for a walk. Cindy told me she had an air ticket for that same day.

"I'll take her tonight. You can leave."

We waited around a while for her to come back so we could say goodbye. But she didn't turn up. So we left.

*

It's Dave Archibald's brother who asked us to tell him the story the other day, because he wanted to turn it into a film script or a book, I don't remember which. We started to tell it, we were both talking over each other, and at a certain point he asked:

"The girl, what was her name?"

I looked at Big Lé. He didn't know any more than I did.

I remembered the road, and the weather, and the guy's face at the border, and the guy who talked to us in the office. I remembered the bridge, I remembered Bezeau and his bad breath, and if I tried, I could have even remembered the name of the motel.

But I'd forgotten the name of the girl.

Lévis said:

"Just call her América. That's all she had to say, anyway."

In the Fields of the Lord
BLOOD SISTERS I

FROM TIME to time, she remembers when her grandmother and Jim were still alive.

Her grandmother was an old village sorceress who believed in St. Elmo's fire, in the devil, in the Holy Trinity, and all sorts of fantastic creatures. She buried saints' medals in the gardens of couples expecting a child, and spat on the lawns of men who beat their wives or forgot to shave before Sunday Mass. She invoked the spirits of the dead, and read the future in playing cards. She died of a heart attack in the village restaurant, in the company of her two oldest friends, while enjoying her favourite pastime, gossip.

Jim was her cousin. He was tall and strong, all his movements were slow and sad, and she was, from her birth, in love with him.

For a long time the three of them had been very happy in the fields of the Lord, then less happy, and then not at all.

From time to time she remembers the little girl she was. She recalls a little girl she once was, but is no more. When she thinks of her grandmother and Jim alive, she can think only about how they died.

From time to time, she remembers.

Once, there was a big family reunion on her parents' land. There must have been a million people under the tents, breathing in the fatty vapours of three spitted lambs revolving over the coals. The little girl wanted to get away from the crowd of children. She saw in the distance the comforting face of her grandmother, and ran towards her with little hopping steps. She embraced her. The old woman was seated sedately on a deck chair, along with other women. She greeted this burst of affection with surprise, but soon began to stroke the little girl's hair, while talking with the other women. Bit by bit, the little girl began to feel uncomfortable. The lady had a strange voice and strange gestures. The lady had a strange smell, and wore a dress she had never seen. The lady was not her grandmother.

She became frightened and started to cry.

The lady disappeared into the crowd and came back with another lady whose face was a duplicate of her own. The little girl stared at the two identical women, and wasn't sure if even one of them was her grandmother. She cried, lashed out, bit all the hands trying to grab hold of her, and fled towards the trees, howling like a little savage. They searched for her until nightfall. Her father found her under a cedar tree, and delicately extricated her with his large farmer's hands. He kissed her on the cheeks, the brow, and at her neck, and explained to her that her grandmother had a twin sister.

When the ambulance had crossed through the village, all its sirens wailing, the little girl had turned to her sister and said:

"It's grandma."

They'd been playing with a box, on the side of the road. In the box, a litter of kittens. There were two grey ones, a black, a pale, two caramels, and a tiger. Her sister had said:

"Don't say that."

But she knew the ambulance was carrying her grandmother, and that her grandmother was going to die.

Her grandmother had had thirteen children, five girls and eight boys. One of them was her father, three were dead, and two were very sick. The little girl got on her bicycle and pedalled up to the old stone house. She knew that her grandmother would not be there that night, and that someone had to bathe her ailing uncles, and tell them a story.

During the funeral, her grandmother's sister planned all the visits to the funeral home in deference to the presence there of the little girl, then almost an adolescent. This was difficult, because the little girl refused to leave her grandmother. She lingered there, half woman and half child. She took a few steps away, sat at the foot of the coffin, or stood covering the dead woman's chill hands, wrapped in a large wooden rosary, with her own warm hands. No one dared to offer her condolences, no one dared to disturb her.

Today she sees in this tale all the wisdom of those people. All the world's wisdom in this tribe putting its own grief on hold out of respect for a child's overweening sorrow. All the world's wisdom in this woman stepping back from her own mourning because the sight of it would be unseemly for a little girl.

The woman had to wait every night for the girl to be coaxed away from her vigil.

From time to time she imagines this woman, alone, watching over her sister in the darkness, while the undertaker cleans up the rooms for the next day. She imagines her also, at home, with her thoughts.

On New Year's Eve, the old woman had gone to the parish church to see the year's dead file out in procession. She had seen her own face pass by, and had returned home in a panic. She calmed down in the days that followed, and put her affairs in order. During the first months of the year she made a point of being pleasant with everybody, and did not often refuse chocolates with cherry filling. She was sad to have to die, but glad to have been forewarned. When the telephone rang and her nephew told her that her sister was dead, she understood right away, and was greatly relieved. Now she felt guilty.

She, Rose-Anna, had not been very close to her sister, Laura-Anna, for thirty years. They lived in neighbouring villages, and never visited each other. That night, however, Rose-Anna found herself dreaming of a time when they were one and the same person, with a single face just like that of the little girl. She dreamed of substituting for the face of her dead sister her own identical face, of adopting the little girl in her turn, and of staying with her until she reached an age when the death of an old woman would no longer affect her to such a degree. Of course, she had her own family and her own children, and nowhere near the energy to embark on such a masquerade. It was only an idea, one of those wild ideas of which insomnias are made, and which in the morning linger on only as a desiccated husk, oak bark and the skin of a snake.

From time to time, she imagines and remembers.

The third night, after the mass and the interment, the little girl was taken to her grandparents'. They had thought that it would do her good to sleep among the scents and belongings of her grandmother. They stretched her out in the wide guest bed, where she went to sleep for the first time in days.

In the middle of the night, she woke. Someone was sitting at the end of the bed. She felt a weight making a hollow in the mattress, and tugging at the bedclothes, right beside her feet. Her grandmother was there in her nightdress, smiling in the lunar half-light, holding out her hand to her, both rough and soft. She was wearing the lavender perfume she reserved for special occasions.

The little girl drew her hand out from under the covers, and stretched it forward. At the last moment she stopped, and closed her fist. The thing made itself even more loving, but it was too late.

Behind the smile, the lavender perfume, and the feigned benevolence, the little girl had seen the rictus, the hideous stench, and absolute evil. She pummelled the air with her feet and fists, and screamed at the dead. The thing rose up. Its night-dress was now a filthy soutane. There was no face. Just bone-white skin, and planted therein two eyes like raisins, contorted by hate. Through the large slits slashed into its neck on each side of its face, the thing hissed like a cat. This time it was neither her grandmother, nor her twin sister, nor the malformed ghost of the little girl they had both once been, but a demon of the fields, an occult force, nemesis to childhood, that seized on the shattered love of young girls to uproot them from the world.

The thing disappeared when the grandfather opened the door and came to take the little girl in his arms. She told him everything. The grandfather himself had become a bit of a sorcerer, out of necessity, through the years. He congratulated her on having defended herself so well, and told her that, had she grasped that hand, the thing would have taken her to a place that was not death, but where no one would want to go.

All week, while mourning her grandmother, she'd sought Jim with her eyes. But she found him nowhere. Months ago he had stopped coming to play cards with the little girl and her grandmother. She would have wanted Jim to take her to where the blueberries were. He would have put on soft music in his car, and opened the windows, and they would have got out to dance, right in the middle of the field. He would have kissed her on the mouth, saying that she was the only one for him, he would have blushed and said that it wasn't good for her to ask him to touch her the same way you touch a woman or that he touched other girls.

The next week, Jim killed himself.

No one knew exactly why. They said he took drugs and owed a lot of money. He came from a village and had never really left it. He didn't know that the world is wide enough for you to hide yourself in it.

He left one night in his car, and parked in their favourite field. It was full of blueberries, and run through with tight rows of black spruce.

Ten years earlier, the little girl's father had brought in a big bulldozer to turn over a section of the field that was full of roots. The bulldozer was old. It broke down, and the operator left it there. For weeks her father called the agricultural equipment company to find out when they'd come to get it. They never came. Her father could have had it towed, but what was the point? Everyone liked the bulldozer a lot. It was a big sculpture in rubber and steel, falling apart in the sun. The shrikes made their nests on the driver's seat, the paint was peeling, the metal rusting, and the machine was sinking into the crumbly soil a bit more each year.

The field was a single long small valley. From where he sat, Jim would have seen endless blueberry stalks, then the bulldozer perched on its mound, the dark wall of trees, and beyond that, the mountaintops.

The blueberry field had its own tragic beauty, but nothing to reassure a young man concerned about the Lord's compassion for his flock. The fields were criss-crossed by insects, mice, field mice, gerbils; on their periphery you could flush out tetras and grouse. They were teeming with so much life that you couldn't take three steps without killing something. The blueberry plants were veritable bonsais clutching at the earth, raked by the seasons, doused, frozen, then buried under tons of snow. Every four years, in autumn, they were burned. In spring the earth was fed with their ashes and they rose from their own graves.

There was nothing in that spectacle to save Jim, but everything to remind him that death and life are nothing, that the world orchestrates each instant the life and death of a billion things, that the living are born from the dead, and the dead give birth to the living, and that no one among the living and the dead is any the worse off for that.

From time to time she asks if, while breathing in carbon monoxide in little gulps, settled into his car, Jim wasn't wanting to come into the world anew.

During the harvest, in the month of August, when the weatherman forecast a freeze, they lit big fires at the corners of the field. The wind made the flames dance and propelled the smoke, which crept in between the plants, enveloped the leaves, and protected the berries from the cold. When the wind was light you had to help it along by shaking big blankets in front of the fires. In the darkness it was like making passes with a cape, veronicas executed right up against the muzzles of great blazing bulls. He might have thought about that, Jim, instead of going out and killing himself. Those people formed a race of builders with heavy feet, unable to settle anywhere without felling a million trees and shooting off guns in all directions. The people were cunning and dumb, tender and cruel, fleshy but strong as horses. You had to see them moving with a matador's grace, dangerously near the big fires, to save the fragile violet berries no bigger than peas, from the freeze. He could have joined with them, Jim, instead of going off to kill himself. Those people could snap a chicken's neck with their bare hands, but they never allowed the delicate things the Lord placed in their care to die.

Not before the harvest, in any case.

Sometimes things are more difficult.

She dares not think of Jim, but she thinks often of her grandmother. Occasionally one of those grey days will come back to her vividly, the way the raw light fell onto the linoleum and the metal legs of the second-hand table, of how good it smelled in the kitchen where they sat to play cards. She remembers the smell of the dishes simmering on the stove, not one in particular but all at the same time, the colour of the walls that was different from now, the children's programs that her afflicted uncles listened to at the other end of the house. The red playing cards swish as they slide across the green plastic tablecloth, a half-consumed cigarette fumes among pistachio shells in the ashtray, the rain taps out a tuneless tune on the dining room windows, but she finds nowhere the face of her grandmother, and sees too late that even this moment, this tiny moment, will never be returned to her.

Every year, in the month of March, she finds herself feeling an infinite sadness for things of no importance, and she rarely wants to make love. The rest of the time, she's happy. She knows the future will be good, that the living and the dead watch over her, and that all will be for the best once more in the fields of the Lord. The cards murmur many things in the ears of people who know how to listen. Her grandmother taught her that a woman has the right to hear what she wants to hear and to leave all the rest suspended from the wings of the birds of affliction.

A Mirror in the Mirror

SHE'D ALWAYS wanted to be blonde, but never dared.

It was only for those creatures who bleached their hair, creatures who wore culottes and cut their hair short. She had dark hair that she wore very long, flowing free, and she would have felt naked without its weighty shadow on the back of her neck. The creatures danced to jazz. Gemma idled at home, tranquil, dreaming of sweeping waltzes that no one danced any more, anywhere.

In any case, the phonograph no longer worked, like many things in this vast dwelling. They had moved there when her father died, to perpetuate the line and take care of her mother. The family had not prospered as a result: her mother had died the following year, and their household remained child-less. Gemma belonged to one of the founding families of the town, of which no trace would soon remain other than this great decrepit house, perched at the top of a cliff that over-looked the town to the west and the lake to the north. She was not ashamed of embodying decadence and extinction, she accepted it philosophically. Everywhere, beyond the sawmill, the paper mill, and the site of the aluminum smelter, the air was alive with modernity, emitting a kind of background noise that was as yet unidentifiable; would it prove to be the grat-ing of metal or a Dixieland melody? The townspeople waited impatiently for the answer, but not her. In either case, it was a music the family would never play.

Michel was away. Michel was a man of the theatre. Gemma's father had welcomed him into the family with reluctance, as one resigns oneself to a fatal illness, knowing that it was certainly not this man who was going to set the family back on the rails, or usher it at last into the twentieth century. But his daughter loved him, and above all Michel loved his daughter, despite her condition. He found her beautiful with her angular features, her paraffin complexion, and her tubercular mien. He liked to see her wandering through the house like the hush between the lines of a romantic poet. So much the better for him.

Michel had promised to return. He'd transferred Gemma's parents' annuity into his own name, and had left to try his luck in Montreal. He'd written several plays which Gemma thought very good, he could act, and there would surely be a place for him in the city. He'd promised to write and to send money. He did neither.

Gemma didn't hold it against him in the least. He had to concentrate on his art. She spent her time dusting and taking care of the garden. The house was enormous and the garden very small, and so she spent more time inside than outside, which was all for the best; when she felt dizzy she sat down in one of the reading room's upholstered armchairs, and gave herself up to daydreams about Michel's success and his imminent return. There wasn't much more to do. The phonograph needle was broken, and she'd read all the books in the house. Sometimes she danced waltzes with herself, her arms crossed, her hands on her shoulders, her head gently tilted to the right, as if offering her neck to be kissed. She could easily imagine the music when she danced, but she tired quickly.

If Michel did not return, it would be a terrible punishment, but a fair one. Michel was not dead set on having children, she knew that, but she also knew from the outset that she could not give him any. She'd lied to him, as she'd hidden the truth from her father. It was a secret she kept to herself, deeply buried: she was not made like other women, she didn't bleed as they did, every month. She had soiled herself, like everyone, around the age of thirteen, but then she had discovered that the bleeding stopped if she took care of herself and ate properly.

Michel's coming, I must make myself stunning. She loved alliteration and naïve rhyme, especially the way it made your tongue quiver against the palate. It tickled.

She had to preserve herself. She went down to the village less and less. The people's faces repelled her, and the walk along the road was long, without horse or car. She cultivated her garden. At first, she had set a few rabbit traps in the nearby woods, but the need to skin them deeply disgusted her, and in truth she hated meat. The vegetable garden produced all she needed, and Gemma put up preserves for the winter. She lived on very little, in any case.

No suitor declared himself during the two years that she waited for Michel, but townsfolk came by occasionally to see how she was. Burly men with shirtsleeves rolled up, along with wives in their Sunday frocks. The men smoked while gazing down at the toes of their boots, and the women asked all sorts of stupid questions, extending invitations that Gemma sometimes had a hard time courteously refusing. Soon she no longer saw anyone, but she awoke from time to time to find pots of food on her doorstep, which she went the same day to empty in the woods before scouring them, her stomach turning, with well water. The intentions were all good, she knew, but it was out of the question for her to eat those fatty soups and those dishes with mud-thick sauces that common people thought fortifying, but that only served to add bulk to a paunch and make women bleed.

You couldn't see the lake from the house, not even from the second floor. From generation to generation the family members had tired of the view, and had let a wall of trees grow up around the point, which had the merit at least of sheltering the house from the wind. Despite this barrier, Gemma sometimes had the feeling, in the depths of winter, that the gusts might raise the house up and heave it stone by stone into the ravenous waters of the lake.

Early in the morning or just before going to bed, she took the road leading towards the town, to where the trees gave way and brought the lake into view. It was an enormous lake, and when the clouds rolled in and shrouded the other shore, it might well have been an ocean. She stood there for a long time, her arms folded, watching the thunderous waves that were invisible from the house.

One day, when she found herself there at dusk, she felt as if a giant hand were lifting her up in its palm, and she let herself be carried off by the wind. For a long time it twirled her about like a cloth ripped from a clothesline, like a poplar leaf, like a speck of dust, just above the lake. She saw herself mirrored in its surface, and for once she found herself beautiful.

When he arrived back in town, Michel did not receive a very warm welcome. He must have been judged severely for his prolonged absence, and perhaps stories were circulating. He took no offence. Soon he would be with Gemma, and for him that was all that counted. There had been no successes in Montreal. Like many failed artists, he had conceded his defeat in small increments, tirelessly repeating to himself the stirring saga of his own genius, prodigious, but misunderstood. He returned, resigned to his wife and his annuity, to contentedly count out the days, and to await posterity in the great empty house that was divorced from a world that had not known how to take his measure.

He bought an enormous bouquet of flowers, and in his enthusiasm, decided to climb the road to the house on foot. By so doing, he spared himself the knowledge that no one would have agreed to give him a ride.

It was not so much his abandonment of Gemma that determined the villagers' reaction to Michel, nor even that it was bruited about that he had applied himself rather lethargically to his artistic ambitions and had squandered his money in the company of a woman whom the prudes spoke of as an actress, but whom the malicious called a whore. Had he been more insightful, not only would Michel have been a better playwright, but he would have seen that the people didn't really hate him, but looked on him rather with an uncommon blend of fear, scorn, and pity.

Madame Nazaire, the butcher's wife, had gone up a few months earlier to retrieve the clean dishes that Gemma left on the doorstep. She found them untouched. Under the towel draped over the broiling pan, the roast beef was crawling with maggots. She left everything the way it was and headed home, driving her team of horses a bit too fast on the long descent.

Monsieur Nazaire made the return trip the next day, after having closed up his butcher's shop, and fetched the dishes. To all the questions his wife and two sons asked him on his return, he replied by slamming his fist on the table. He left the kitchen without having touched his plate, and sat himself down in the living room, in his armchair, where he drank enough small glasses of De Kuyper to empty half a bottle. Before going to sleep, he said to his wife:

"We'll have to tell everyone never to go up there again."

Now that he seemed calm, Madame Nazaire was able to say to him:

"You know, if she's dead, we'll have to tell the police."

He turned his back, stretched out his hand to turn down the oil lamp, and grumbled in the half-light:

"She's not dead."

She was often seen after that, at the curve in the road from where she looked down on the lake. But from such a distance, she couldn't be identified with certainty. It could also have been a long black dress hooked onto a post and lifted by the wind.

Michel entered the house, put his suitcase down on a bench in the hall, and walked towards the reading room calling out to Gemma, his big bouquet of flowers in his hand.

She didn't come. From the dining room, out of the corner of his eye, he thought he could make out her silhouette in the kitchen. He quickened his pace and burst through the doorway, to surprise her. She wasn't there. He climbed the stairs, and thought he heard her moving around in one of the bedrooms. He negotiated the corridor in long strides, and found all the rooms empty. He repeated her name, loudly, retraced his steps, and passed in front of the bathroom door. He stopped cold.

He had seen her, in front of the mirror, shockingly thin, her face hidden behind her dark hair, which she was brushing in short strokes. But Gemma wasn't in the bathroom. The brush was there, lying on the dressing table, there were also a few hairs in the bottom of the bathtub, and Michel even detected, hanging in the air, the scent of that heady perfume she adored, but that didn't suit her.

He looked for her for a long time. He paced the house, opening doors and calling her name. He often glimpsed her slender silhouette at the other end of a room, but it vanished as soon as he fixed his eyes on it. He persevered long after he had realized that this was not a game, long after it had far surpassed the scope of the simply strange, because he didn't see what else he could do.

One night, dozing in his armchair, he was awakened by a smell. Gemma was there, before him, very close. His head was bowed and he saw her only as far as her chest. She put her hand in his. The hand was neither warm nor cold. It might have been a set of knucklebones enclosed in a thin suede bag. She said:

"Look at me."

He gave a start, perhaps woke, and made a decision. He rose, went to the bathroom, shaved, took a bath, and lay down on the bed. He had eaten nothing for three days.

The next day, he went down to the village and shopped. He then cleaned the house from top to bottom, removed the shutters that no one had taken off in the spring, and opened all the windows. The rooms had been plunged in darkness for so long that the light, almost gaseous, penetrated slowly, rolling over itself like a drop of blood fallen in water.

Michel began to write and to sleep in the master bedroom. After a few weeks, the villagers began to ask him questions. A few inquired hypocritically after Madame Gemma, others dared to ask him if he intended to leave the manor house and remake his life. As usual, the people in town understood nothing.

Gemma was in the house. With him. She lived now on the periphery of his gaze, behind half-open doors, and in the depths of mirrors.

As long as she was there, he would have no reason to leave.

The Animal
BLOOD SISTERS II

COLOUR HAD not yet returned to the world but the light was already there like a thick coat of primer blearing the surface of things. Frogs were croaking in the pond and birds were beginning to sing in the branches of distant trees. It wasn't quite day and it was no longer night, it was a part of the day that belonged to no one and her father poked his head through the half-open door to say in a soft voice:

"Wake up, my babies."

She heard her sister groaning in her bed on the other side of the room. She still couldn't see anything. Her eyes had adjusted neither to the darkness nor the faint light filtering between the curtains. To her half-shut eyes the room looked like a Polaroid, with all the posters and all the furniture and all the curios in the same place as the night before, except for her sister who had gone to sleep facing her, her arms over her breasts and her delicate fists clasped under her chin as if in prayer, but who was now lying on her back with one arm across her face.

"Lucy, wake up."

Her sister moaned.

After their father, their mother looked in with her voice that was sometimes piercing and sometimes high-pitched and sometimes low and threatening but never soft. Her mother had a husband and five daughters and two dogs and seven chickens and three rabbits and an indeterminate number of cats. She had a house to run and not much time to be gentle, especially in the morning.

The little girl who really wasn't one, the adolescent, sat up in bed and began to stretch. There wasn't a muscle or a nerve or an organ of her body that was not howling that it wanted to go back to sleep but she'd decided it wasn't to be and she stuck to her guns. She got on all fours and extended her neck and arms and back just like a cat, making little orbits with her shoulders. She arched and de-arched, bringing her head forward and back as far as she could go in each direction.

"Lucie, get up before mama arrives."

Her sister groaned again.

"Okay, then sleep. Big ninny."

There was not a muscle not a nerve and not an organ that wasn't pleading with her to stop this torture and go back between the sheets where she would be sheltered from the cold, where her entrails would stop wrenching and tearing and twisting in her belly like the gears of an archaic machine. But she didn't stop and didn't listen to the voices and did not go back under the covers. The adults were always comparing themselves to animals. They said they were strong as horses, smart as mice or sparrows, fearful as hares. They were pig-headed or had faces like cows. They tried to set themselves apart as well. She liked her parents because they often spoke more kindly about animals than people. They respected animals and said while reading the newspaper or watching television, "A dog wouldn't do that," or "A horse wouldn't do that." But they were exceptional. The others lay in wait for an animal's instinct to betray it so they could scoff at its stupidity. It seemed to be an ordeal for them to see love in the eyes of a dog or their own expressions on the face of a monkey.

She knew exactly what differentiated men from animals and she knew the difference was very slight and had nothing to do with love or sadness or the capacity of people to feel whatever it was but everything to do with their ability to deny emotions the right to run rampant within them. Man was not the only intelligent creature but he was the only one who could use his intelligence to no longer feel and to no longer be a creature at all. She knew all that and she trained herself not to heed what issued from her heart and her innards. She was training herself this very moment by extricating herself from under the covers despite the supplications of her every cell. Soon she would experience everything but would allow herself to be touched by nothing and she would be not at all animal but totally man, totally woman.

She accused her sister several more times of being dense and dumb for not being able to get out of bed, but their mother didn't come to shout at them from the bedroom doorway and when the adolescent and her now wakened sister burst into the kitchen, she stopped them short, saying:

"Sit down. What do you want for breakfast?"

"We can't have breakfast, mama. We'll be late."

"No. Papa doesn't want you to walk today. He's going to drive you. You want eggs?"

The girls sulked a little, then ate in silence.

The girls loved going to work on foot because they had to cross what they called the fields of the Lord up to Concession Road 3, and Monsieur Béliveau's fields as far as the gravel road serving the residents of Lac Brochet, and follow the road for a hundred metres before turning right onto the dirt road that had belonged to the hydroelectric company and wound its way through the hills up to the cadet camp. It took almost an hour every morning but they loved doing it together at dawn. Their grandfather had been a guard at the hydroelectric company's installation. He'd spent half his life tramping these roads and the girls felt that the road was theirs and that the whole world belonged to them when they walked on it. It was an ancient world where an old broken-down shelter became a castle's ruins. An imaginary world they peopled with creatures they didn't believe in but that they'd believed in for long enough that the bushes and crevices along the way remained forever their lairs. They imagined imps and fairies, dragons and werewolves; they imagined enormous creatures that were half fish and half reptile and that swam in the brackish current of the little stream, and the girls even contrived to see them forcing their way through the water's surface with powerful strokes of their fins.

There was also a real cowboy.

The handsome Monsieur Robertson sometimes rode one of his horses along the road at dawn and they played a game with him. Always the same. It was a game that never changed. A ritual. They whistled at Monsieur Robertson every time they met or passed him along the road and they said "Howdy, cowboy," assuming the provocative poses of saloon molls while he greeted them by pinching the brim of his hat and saying, "Med'moiselles." He didn't look like their father who was short in stature, both sturdy and portly.

He was tall and gnarled but his face betrayed the same mix of gentleness and strength as did that of their father, something they didn't find in most of the men their father resembled.

This was their path through a world that belonged to them only and they hated it when a car passed by or when their father drove them because as far as they were concerned fairies could perfectly well rub shoulders with cowboys but not with Cadillacs, and for them such machines were huge metal blots on the landscape. But Billy had come back and their father didn't want them wandering around out in the open so he'd decided that they would spend this morning on a dreary road behind the windows of a pick-up truck that like a dull blade strips the world of all its mystery and magic.

★

One Sunday a long time ago their father had come to pick them up in his truck and said to them:

"Get in, my babies."

Lucie was fourteen and she was twelve. They didn't like being seen in public with their parents any more, but the Sunday excursions still held sway to some extent. They often amounted to a simple tour of the fields of the Lord and the village streets, but sometimes they turned into something else. When they were little that's how their trips began. Their father loaded up the baggage in secret and came to fetch them in the car with their mother and they drove all four together or all five once Angèle was born or all six once Frédérique was born or all seven once Corinne was born, and their mother turned to them with, in the palm of her hand, two doses of Gravol, one for each of them, and they woke up somewhere else. In the house of strangers or on roads they didn't know.

Once their father had asked them:

"Would you like to see the ocean, my babies?"

And he had led them through valleys and across mountains to the great river where they had boarded a boat and seen lazy whales like big boulders just peeking out of the water.

Once their father had asked them:

"Would you like to fly in the sky, my babies?"

And they had driven to a nearby airfield and their father had taken them for a ride in a Cessna with a pilot friend. They had flown over their house on the fields of the Lord, and flown farther over fields and houses and lakes and kilometres of forest. The girls had the feeling that the world was much bigger than they would have believed but also smaller because they could with one bent index figure encircle whole villages. From the sky the world was like a miniature model but when they arrived face on to the brilliant sun over the limitless Lac Saint-Jean, the little girls, blinded, lost all notion of geography, and they believed like the pagans that there existed nothing beyond the lake and that they had come to the end of something.

That Sunday their father had asked, once they were both settled in the back seat:

"Do you want to see a bear, my babies?"

The girls had already seen horses and cows and hares and frogs and all sorts of animals including the eagle owl that had amused itself for months opening the skulls of their mother's cats to peck away at the insides of their heads, consuming the contents like a sorbet. The girls had always had cats and dogs and they had seen hundreds of insects and had extricated from the muddy edges of the trout pond black and yellow salamanders they kept in a tortoise aquarium and they had even seen a fox once at the back of a blueberry field and a moose on the cadet camp road, but the only bears they had seen were in their imaginations.

Their father took them with him in the autumn to put up electric fences around the beehives. The odour of honey attracted bears and you had to protect the hives from their attacks. It was just a precaution because there were not many bears around but the girls liked to believe in danger and their father let them do so. They imagined the silhouettes of mammoths writhing and roaring at the edge of the forest with red eyes and frothy mouths and big yellow fangs. Those monsters were all they knew of bears.

Their father led them to an old farmhouse behind which there was no longer a farm but just a big shed and an old lopsided barn and the carcass of an ancient tractor. Behind the shed there was a cage as big as the shed itself. It was two metres high and its rectangular surface was fifteen metres by ten. The wooden structure was made from big square-ended beams. Six of them were planted like pickets; four marked out the limits of the structure and two reinforced it at the mid-points of the longer sides. Other beams were installed horizontally to form a frame at the end and in the middle of each support. Between the beams there was metal mesh as in a chicken coop but with wider openings, and steel strands that were much thicker. In the cage was a large mound of black fur glinting blue that was pacing to and fro and sniffing the ground. From a distance you might have thought it was a dog but the animal was bigger and it smelled stronger and its eyes were both gentler and wilder and its muzzle looked made out of wood. A man came out of the house. He shook their father's hand and kissed both girls on their cheeks and ushered them into the cage where they could pet the chained-up bear. Its fur was thicker and stiffer than that of a dog and underneath its body seemed warmer. The old gentleman stayed next to the bear while they were touching it and stroking its neck and said in its ear that it was a good bear and a good animal and talked to it just like you talk to a horse or a dog.

*

On the way home their father told them that the old man's name was Monsieur Roberge. He'd been a friend of their grandfather and had become his own friend when he'd hired him to help build his house. Monsieur Roberge had been an avid hunter all his life and deep down he still was even though he hadn't hunted for years. You call an avid hunter like Monsieur Roberge a Nemrod, which was the name of a great hunter in the Bible. It was hard to understand for little girls like them, but people who kill animals often love animals dearly, and it's hard to grasp but a Nemrod like Monsieur Roberge had to his credit only a limited number of kills. Never mind his skill in tracking and flushing out and trapping game, one day a Nemrod could no longer muster the strength to kill it.

Monsieur Roberge was at just that point when he'd met Billy. He'd not killed for years and went to his camp just to fish and prepare the hunting grounds for his sons. He set up salt licks and dug mud holes and scattered apples and at day's end called deer and moose. He took animal photos. He never told anyone, but he sometimes got close enough to the moose to touch them.

One night their garbage can, which they kept outside with a heavy stone on the lid, was overturned and the plastic bag inside was torn open and the contents were scattered all about. To reassure Madame Roberge, Monsieur Roberge blamed it on racoons and their legendary cleverness but he began to check the surroundings looking for clues. The ground was dry and there were no tracks and by the time he saw them the shed had been smashed into and the refrigerator door torn off and what remained of the provisions and plastic wrappings and chicken bones and shattered Mason jars was spread everywhere around the house and you couldn't hold racoons responsible for that. On his satellite phone he called a game warden he knew and asked his advice. The warden said:

"If there's a bear that's fallen in love with your garbage you'd best kill it. He'll never get tired of visiting you and one fine day he'll come when your wife is all alone picking mushrooms or your grandchildren are there for the weekend and you know as well as I do how something like that can end up."

Monsieur Roberge had heard about relocating bears. The agents captured a bear in a trap and went to free it at the ends of the earth.

"But you're already at the ends of the earth. Where will we put it, your bear? You do that for bears that get near urban spaces or rural communities. We could try it with your bear but that would just pass the problem on to another hunter."

Monsieur Roberge said he understood and he hung up.

The next day he hung from the branches of trees, in every direction, rags impregnated with vanilla extract, and he laid out bait by distributing pails of stale doughnuts and rotten fruit and bacon grease here and there on the property. Then he sat in an old bus seat on his steps and cleaned and loaded his rifle and waited, calm and motionless. An hour passed and then two and then three and in the middle of the fourth hour, at dusk, the bear came out of the woods about thirty metres from the house. It had smelled him but it had also smelled the pail of bait sitting in front of it and it hesitated. The bear looked both ways in the clearing like a child crossing the street. When it turned its head the other way Monsieur Roberge, who had killed nothing and taken aim at nothing for years, shouldered the gun and buried a hundred-and-eighty-grain bullet in its vital parts, tearing in two the bear's big heart. The bear took ten steps. For the first five it seemed normal and just frightened by the explosion. At the sixth it seemed to be running on ice. At the tenth its legs gave way beneath it as if its four kneecaps had dislocated at the same time. It had come near enough to the house for Monsieur Roberge to see a laborious breath swell its flank. He reloaded and heard the ejected cartridge bounce off the wooden porch. Madame Roberge, who didn't like to see animals killed, had stayed inside the house. From behind the screen she asked:

"Is it over?"

"Yes. Please bring me my knives."

He went down the steps with his rifle in his hands. The bear was no longer breathing. He circled the body and thrust the gun's barrel into the bear's glassy eye. It was then that he heard the little growls and saw the small animal come out of the woods at the exact spot from which its mother had emerged. Instinctively Monsieur Roberge took off the rifle's safety catch even though he already knew that he'd never have the heart to kill it.

His wife arrived a few minutes later with the knives. She approached cautiously and asked her husband, whose back was turned:

"Is he dead?"

"She's dead," he said, turning around with the animal in his arms.

The cub whimpered and nibbled and sucked the ends of his fingers as if they were nipples. It didn't really hurt.

"What's that?"

"That is my bear."

The girls asked dozens of questions when they got home.

"How did they feed it?

"The Roberges had an old golden retriever, Jackie. She nursed and weaned Billy like a pup."

"Really?"

"I swear."

"Is he tame?"

"About as tame as a bear can be."

"Are we going to go back to see him?"

"Yes my babies, but you mustn't mention it to anyone. Monsieur Roberge doesn't have the right to keep a bear."

But of course word spread after a few years and Billy had reached an age where nothing, not his cage nor his chain, could hold him, and the warden put Monsieur Roberge's back up against the wall, offering to relocate the bear. Twice they'd tried and twice the bear had found his way back. The first time he'd ransacked the Gauthiers' garbage and the second time he'd killed and eaten the Langlois' dog. Ten days earlier they'd tried a third time and had transported it a great distance and that's why their father had insisted on driving them. He sensed that it would be back soon.

That morning they kept on asking questions as if this conversation was an extension of the other and as if not two seconds had passed in the two years that separated them from the first day they'd met Billy.

"What did they do with him?"

"They led him far into the forest, so far that he'll never find his way back, and he'll stay there."

"Do you think it will work?"

"No."

"Why?"

"It's hard to explain."

"What will they do if he comes back?"

"Nothing. They'll put him back in his cage and try again."

"You're lying, papa."

He smiled and stopped the truck in front of the cadet camp's sentry box. The guard, a zealous redhead with a bad case of acne, inspected them as if they were potential terrorists. Their father looked at Lucie on the passenger seat and looked at the adolescent in the back seat and then his gaze came to rest somewhere between the two.

"It's hard to understand, but Billy's no longer afraid of men, and an animal that's lost its fear of men is a dangerous animal. If Billy comes back Monsieur Roberge will have to kill him."

The mess was located in a log building with the kitchens at the back separated from the cafeteria by a stainless steel counter and a line of hot plates. The girls served from behind and the cadets passed in front in single file before going to sit at one of the twenty tables arranged in two rows. There were a hundred and thirty cadets and twenty or so instructors to feed morning, noon and night, and they were five in the kitchen plus the caretaker who sometimes lent a hand. There were the adolescent, Lucie, the manager Madame Rosie, and her two daughters. The younger, Cynthia, was eighteen and she was normal, but the older, Monique, was thirty-eight and she was retarded. Between the two Madame Rosie had had four sons who'd all left home, something Cynthia dreamed of doing one day, while Monique never strayed far without fear and trembling.

Monique couldn't do all the work like the others but she was good at repetitive tasks and her mother even let her cut vegetables with a knife as long as she kept up her pace because when she did so she was not likely to hurt herself. Madame Rosie knit little wool shawls and cardigans that she left hanging on a nail beside the cold room, and insisted that anyone who went with her into the refrigerator or the freezer put one on.

"Go into the cold like that in the middle of summer and you come out with a runny nose!"

But sometimes she herself cheated, just draping a bit of wool over her shoulders before making a quick visit.

The five together had to wash and peel and prepare and cook and roast and simmer and serve all sorts of dishes. It was hard work, very hard, and they amused themselves as best they could. As the cadets paraded in front of them with their trays the girls greeted them with the same poses and the same come-hither glances they reserved for their cowboys, but the cadets didn't have Monsieur Robertson's poise and they blushed and stammered and sometimes spilled their soup or dessert and Madame Rosie laughed until tears came to her eyes and she called the girls "my little devils."

They never flirted seriously with the cadets. The cadets were a subnormal and weak and insignificant species. It wasn't healthy at their age to need so badly to obey and be obeyed, to be served and to be servile. They cherished the memory of their cousin Jim who'd been a ne'er-do-well and who'd killed himself the year before. They thought that a good-looking boy their age ought like Jim to be a good-for-nothing and a bit of a scoundrel and not a little play soldier. For them to be interested in one of them he'd have to have less acne and be better looking than the others, but above all he'd have to be his own person whom they could imagine alone on a horse or a motorcycle and not a pallid figure surrounded by a big platoon of imbeciles. The girl cadets were no better. They got crushes on stupid boys and tried to look tough and their khaki pants gave them big behinds and to the girls they were just beefy ugly ducklings.

That day the adolescent wasn't laughing and wasn't in a mood for play. She was thinking of Billy who'd never frightened her and whom she'd have liked to meet on the road and she was sad for him and she was praying to the good Saint Anne for him not to return, but above all she was afraid, afraid of the fear she'd have to stroke that night like a big cat rolled into a ball on her stomach and the fear in her belly like nausea itself.

The warden had put Billy into his cage and with his helper had hoisted the cage onto the back of the truck. Monsieur Roberge had whispered a few words into the bear's ear. And then they'd hit the road.

The three of them had passed through Canton-Tremblay and had driven along the Saguenay and crossed Chicoutimi-Nord and Saint-Fulgence de l'Anse-aux-Foins and had advanced into the mountains until they saw Stone Consolidated's huge mounds of wood. They'd turned left onto the Controlled Zone road and had stopped at the registration office to show the bear. Only one of the gamekeepers came out, because he hadn't seen the bear the first two times. Slowly they proceeded along the gravel road across the Monts-Valin hills and passed the lakes le Savard, le Barbu, la Rotule, le Jalobert, le Louis, le Charles, le Victor, le Breton, le Betsiamites, le Marie, le Gilles, and they turned left just before the Tagï River and went on to the Portneuf River camp where they stopped to pee and to show the bear to the woodcutters. After, they drove for another hour and a half until they were in the middle of nowhere in another sector far from the woodsmen and the hunters. Spread out before them were wide valleys covered in new growth and moss and grey, emaciated skeletons of trees that had escaped the clear cutting but had not survived it. They tranquillized Billy again and they pulled out the cage and lowered it from the truck. Billy growled weakly and you could tell he was angry but that he had no more strength left in him. He lay down next to the road after having taken a few uncertain steps. The warden removed his collar and chain and passed his hand through the fur on his head and down between his shoulder blades and he and his helper left with hours of road in front of them as the sun began its descent over the broken line separating the horizon from the highest mountains.

It was almost night when Billy came out of his stupor. He grazed on the plants and currants and blueberries around him and then set out. He felt very far away but he sniffed the ground just in case. He'd find a trail sooner or later. He had nothing against these woods. There was lots to eat and space to move around in and plenty of animals and things to entertain him along the way.

He walked for days and days.

There was in his bear's soul an ancestral knowledge of the cardinal points and nutritional needs and the seasonal cycle and a certain violence but in his bear's head he didn't know solitude and above all he didn't know that it was normal for a bear not to have a house.

"What's the matter?"

They were outside. The adolescent was at the edge of the trout pond. Their father had widened the stream that flowed past the house, and built little stone walls around it. Some of the passing trout lingered there and you could see them sleeping in shadow during the day. At night the little girl sat by the water and let her feet dangle. Their mother gave her a hot dog and with her thumbnail she broke off little lumps and threw them into the pool. For a few moments the small pieces made bright spots on the black water and slowly sank towards the bottom before being snapped up by the trout. You could guess where the trout were, seeing the bits of sausage disappear or suddenly veer off inexplicably.

"What's the matter?"

"Nothing."

The screen door slammed and the dog barked where he lay beside the garage.

"What's the matter?"

"Nothing, I said."

They turned towards the house. Their father was walking in their direction and all at once he stopped and there was a loud report. He turned his head towards the row of trees that cut the property in two at the right of the house and stared into space for a moment as if wanting to see past what was there.

"Do you want to see Billy one last time, my babies?"

Lucie didn't answer and ran past her father into the house. The adolescent said:

"I'll go with you."

The old man was facing away from them on his knees beside the bear, which lay on its side. They got out of the car and approached slowly. Their father cleared his throat. The old man didn't turn around but raised a hand in the air and signalled for them to come.

"Come here, my lovely girl."

The adolescent moved forward and placed her hand in the old man's hand, both rough and moist. He led her as for a waltz to the other side of the bear, facing him, and invited her to kneel as well and guided her small hand into the thick fur under which the bear's body was still warm and haunted by the echo of a heartbeat.

"Pat him."

The old man turned around and stood and walked up to their father who said:

"So there was still one more kill in you."

"There's always one more."

"I'm sorry."

"For what?"

"That you had to kill him."

"Don't be. I made it happen. The day I took Billy. If I'd left him there the good Lord would have killed him and when I saved him I took his life into my hands and I knew I'd find myself here. I knew I was the one who'd have to kill him and that's how things had to happen because by saving his life I'd agreed to be God for him. Don't be more sorry for me than for God who counts each of our hairs and kills us all one day or another. You can't be sorry for me any more than you can be sorry for God, any more than you can blame us or pardon us. That's been turning around in my head. For about ten years. I'd talked to my wife about it. She was a God-fearing woman, my wife, and I asked her why in a religion where they talk so much about forgiveness there's no ritual for forgiving God. She said, 'What do you mean?' and I explained 'It's God's fault if his son suffered. He's responsible for children having no father and parents ruined by their children and battered women and women being raped and he's responsible for all the wars and the dead soldiers and the maimed. Nothing happens on earth that he doesn't cause or that he doesn't allow to happen so why do we never try to forgive him?' She told me I'd committed a terrible blasphemy and she made me promise never to repeat it anywhere and I promised but the next week I asked the same question to the priest at confession. He told me the same thing as my wife: 'There's no point in my giving you any Hail Marys but I'm going to pray for you and you'd do well to ask all the people you know to do the same.' I still said what I thought. I think people don't talk about it because in a religion where you have to forgive everybody you can't mention God's name when you talk about forgiveness. You can praise him and sing

for him but you can't ever say anything about his most important attribute which is to be unforgivable. Everyone has his reasons except him because he's the one who decides what's what
and he's the only one who can make things happen differently.
It's the same thing for Billy and me on a smaller scale and it's
the same thing for you and your girls. You're the whole world
for them and you knew when they were born everything that
might happen to them and that you'd have no excuses to give
them and you'd have to be responsible for everything. Our
brothers and our sisters who are idiots and understand nothing they can always say they didn't know and they didn't do it
on purpose and it's not their fault and people will forgive them
because they're just the same. But we're the clever ones and
people know it and you can never say it's not our fault because
those with the knowledge are never forgiven."

Their father shook his head.

"I don't know anything about anything. Especially not
what you're talking about."

The old man kissed the little girl on the top of her head
and walked towards the little halo of light over the back door.

Their father said "Come my beauty, we're going," and
she ran to the car without looking at him and like Monsieur
Roberge without looking at the bear.

In the car her father cleared his throat several times. He
hummed and cleared his throat again. All along the way the
adolescent repeated in her head: "Don't talk don't talk please
don't talk." They only saw the trees and the telephone poles
and the houses and garages and barns in silhouette and the
night was an incandescent black light that shone on things just
enough to hide them behind their shadows and its work was
complete except for a few naked bulbs aglow over the lintels.

She knew what he would have said.

He would have said:

"The world is a hard place for men and maybe worse for women and it's hard for a man to bring children into it and maybe even worse if they're girls. You can show boys all you know and hope they'll handle things just like you did but girls are delicate things and it's tempting for a father never to teach them anything and to hope nothing will ever happen to them and to try to protect them from the world instead of showing them how to live in it."

All during the ride she repeated "Don't talk, papa," because if he'd talked she'd have had to tell him that she'd learned all that a long time ago all on her own and his silence hadn't protected her from anything.

When they got back to the house everyone was sleeping and cats were lying here and there in the darkness and the TV's blue glow was pulsing and in fits and starts turning their grey fur a bit paler. In the half-light the grandfather clock tolled midnight and the little girl was limp with a fatigue that kept her from sleeping and she knew that the next day she'd be dizzy and would have a stomach ache but she was fine with that because she didn't want to sleep right away. She brushed her teeth and left the bathroom to her father and wished him good night. In her room she let her jeans drop to her ankles and pulled off her socks and her sweater. She undid her brassiere and let it fall to the ground and with her nails scratched the moist undersides of her breasts. Lucie hadn't moved or talked and her breathing was deep.

She lay down on her side to look at her sister. She didn't want to wake her but it felt good to see her on the other side of the room.

When she was very little she'd often had the same dream. She was in a familiar place like her room and she was playing with a doll or petting a cat and all at once the door behind her slammed and the room got small and in her arms the cat was dead and from under her button eyes the doll was weeping blood. Something enormous was moving in the closet and the doorknob was turning and slowly the door opened, creaking on its hinges. She always woke up before having seen what was stirring in the darkness. If she'd had those dreams later that would have explained it but she'd had them well before so it must have been a sort of premonition because that's how things happened precisely. She always felt safe when he appeared and in a flash there were no more escape routes. Nothing stirred in the closet because she wasn't always in her room, sometimes she was in the garage or out in the fields but there was nowhere to run to, nothing in the closet but inside him there was something that rasped and seethed. He looked a lot like her father and as with many men who looked like her father there was neither the same softness nor the same strength in his face and in his eyes.

She was not sure of having tried one day not to struggle and not to flee and not to be afraid. She remembered one time but perhaps she was imagining it because she's the little girl now. She's living in her dream and she's lying inside it swathed in a little pink nightie hiked over her hips and he's in front of her on his knees beside the bed and on the other side of the room her sister is looking at her with dead eyes and all the doors are locked and thick boards are nailed across the windows.

With one finger, then two, he slips into the hollow of her womb a shameful warmth. As always he's gentle with her and as always he's careful not to rush her and not to hurt her. As always he leaves no mark on her body and no scar, only on her skin the flush of an inscrutable pleasure and shame in her heart. Shame she tries to throw off as always all alone hidden deep in herself but suddenly someone's behind her in the bed and her arms are slender and her breasts are warm pressed up against her back. She's known boys and she'll know others but it's her sister who is the first to murmur in her ear "my love" and to repeat "my love" until she's calmed.

Her grandmother when she was alive was not afraid to reveal secrets and terrible truths.

To honour an ancient custom they had placed at the edge of the village a high wooden cross on a stone pedestal to hold the devil at bay. The township was big, however, and many were the villagers who lived on unhallowed land.

The grandmother didn't believe that the devil had residence in America. She did see him implanted where he was born in Europe along with Communists and Protestants. She said that the cross was useful all the same to protect them from the little gods who had come to America in boat holds or who were already there at the time of the Indians. The grandmother had talked to her a lot about those spiteful gods that reigned as despots on parcels of land of no more than a few acres. They were bonded to the earth, and their aspect changed according to the seasons. They were robust in spring and alluring in summer and not far from obese just before harvest but when winter moved in to dislodge autumn they began to waste away. They hid themselves, grey shadows on snow, behind bushes and their hair fell out and their eyes sank deep into their orbits and they could no longer close their mouths completely over their pointed teeth. They were the earth and relied on the earth and served the earth. They worshipped the sun and at twilight they dreamed up ghoulish dances to bring down the rain.

They knew the earth needed light and water but also blood. They were the ones who sometimes sucked blood from the necks of cows and ripped out their viscera in a cruel game and left mutilated bodies lying there so the crimes would be blamed on extraterrestrials or wolves. They were haughty and sadistic and even if their names were forgotten and no one believed in them, they demanded sacrifices from the infidels.

They stole from houses what was their due as offerings and whispered their rage and desires into sleepers' ears at night so that the earth might obtain in good time all it thirsted for.

With her sister behind her murmuring "my love" she realizes that to her too he'd said that what was happening to her would not happen to her sisters and that she was the single chosen one. With her sister at her back murmuring "my love" she realizes that they had been sacrificed both of them on the altar of the minor gods and that this sacrifice had saved neither one nor the other. In this house and in the other houses of the township, on the hallowed land of the village and beyond the tall cross, everyone is sleeping and everyone's eyes are closed.

*

The light had not totally left the world but the sun yes and the brightness was like a memory of itself that likened everything to its own imprint on a poorly exposed piece of film. The adolescent was walking with the dogs on the fields of the Lord between the roads that framed the blueberry plantings. For hours she'd been looking for tracks. With darkness coming on she now knew she'd find no more.

She went back to the house. Lucie was sick in bed. She'd got a runny nose from going into the camp refrigerators without her wool scarf. The adolescent got undressed and lay down to watch her sleep. Lucie had a big compress over her forehead and eyes and she rasped as she breathed.

For several days she'd been hearing the wolf at night as it howled outside. Those were the tracks she was looking for and she'd found some but she knew they were dog tracks. No one was talking about the wolf and no one had heard the wolf except her, who even thought she could understand its baying. Every night, far, very far beyond the borders of the village, past the railway line and the rock quarry, the wolf howled and said to her "When the time comes, when I'll have decided, you'll go mad."

The people in the village were not like the animals and they didn't expel the weakest members of the pack. They kept the demented in houses and fed them but everyone looked at them as if they were dead, with death in their eyes. She didn't want to be gazed at like that. She didn't ever want to go mad and she did everything she could under the covers, plugging her ears so as not to hear the baying of the wolf.

At the foot of the bed, between her legs, she felt a weight pulling on the quilt and flattening the mattress. A little girl was sitting there and looking at her.

The little girl said:

"He doesn't touch us any more because when you get older you become fat and ugly."

"No, it's because I'm becoming a woman."

"Little girls like me always go mad."

"No. Not if they're not afraid of being afraid any more, not if they become like me, an animal that refuses to let itself be touched or to let itself die or to let itself be caught. Me, I'm going to run in my dreams until no one can find me.".

"You won't succeed."

"There are afternoons when he didn't catch us and you know it. I'm dreaming of those now."

"At the gates of the town a wolf is howling and you're the only one to hear it. You're already mad."

"You don't understand. The wolf is with me. He's protecting me from monsters and little gods and you."

The little girl said:

"Idiot. He's come to devour us."

"Yes, but he won't let anyone do it except for him."

The day was going to be hard with two hands less but Friday was the day for junk food. The cadets ate Pogos and poutine and pizzas and there was less work for the women in the kitchen.

She left the house alone at dawn and alone crossed the fields of the Lord up to the Third Line and walked alone through Monsieur Béliveau's fields and along Lac Brochet's gravel road. Autumn was coming early and the nights were cold but the August sun that rose over the dew was as warm as that of July and this afternoon it would shine incongruously on the red leaves and the tree branches drained of all their sap.

She'd not taken a hundred steps along the hydroelectric company road when she heard behind her a horse's hooves striking the hard-packed ground. She stayed where she was to let the horse pass. Monsieur Robertson stopped beside her. He was wearing his beautiful white hat and black leather pants and a brand new white shirt and was mounted on his handsomest horse, solid black. Together they seemed to have escaped overnight from an old cowboy film and of having trotted that far without any notion at dawn that this was a world of colour.

"Bonjour, Mad'moiselle."

"Bonjour, Monsieur Robertson."

"You're all alone?"

"Yes. My sister's sick."

"Ah."

He looked at her and looked at the ground and looked at her again and turned and spat on the ground.

"Good day, then."

"Good day."

The horse and rider moved on. They went thirty metres at a walk and then turned and came back at a trot. Monsieur Robertson stopped his horse just in front of her in the road.

"I guess no one's ever arrived at the cadet camp on horseback?"

"Never."

He smiled.

"Come, climb on up."

He shifted his weight and lifted one leg in the air so she could put her foot in the stirrup and he held out his arm and helped her to swing from left to right into the saddle. She moved her pelvis around a bit before finding a comfortable position.

"Is that all right?"

"Yes."

She stretched her arms around him and he clicked his tongue and the horse began to advance at a walk and then at a trot. After a few minutes, Monsieur Robertson asked:

"Do you want to gallop?"

"Yes."

"Hang on tight."

He struck the horse's sides with the heels of his boots and the horse altered its pace and went faster and faster. She felt the horse's body working beneath her and for a fraction of a second all three of them were hurtling through the air and a moment later hitting the ground and she felt as if she were caught in the midst of a struggle between two ancient forces, one that distanced them from the ground and the other that pulled them back and she felt that the ground and the earth beneath her were trying to strike at her through the horse but the horse was absorbing the shock with its body to protect her from the blows.

Monsieur Robertson turned his head a little and cried:

"Are you afraid?"

She wrapped her arms around him a bit tighter and said:

"No."

自害 (Jigai)

THE MEN SAY:

She came from the ends of the earth with pebbles in her pockets.

We never knew anything else. Very little, in any case.

She came from the ends of the earth with pebbles in her pockets, and she lived for a while in the boarding house of Akira Gengei, the innkeeper. He knew her best. But very little, he says. He does know that back there, where she came from, things happened to her that shouldn't happen to a woman and especially not a child. He says he doesn't know why she came here, and probably neither does she. After, she bought old Mifune's house and we never learned anything more.

We don't much like foreigners around here, but even if this was before the war, there was already a fascination, in the cities and the countryside, for the West. For America, especially.

She made a place for herself. We never knew if she truly became a subject of the Empire, but after a while she had herself called Misaka. Because she never gave any other name. And since soon the people of Sapporo and Asahikawa began to send young people her way to board with her during the summer so they'd learn America's customs and languages, we all began to call her Misaka-sensei.

She'd come from the ends of the earth and she'd landed here, on the peninsula.

Did she know that *Shiretoko*, in the language of the Ainus, meant just that, "the ends of the earth?"

Misaka says:

I came from the ends of the earth with pebbles in my pockets.

They may have told you so. They may have added that *Shiretoko* means "ends of the earth," but they are mistaken. My host, Akira Gengei, was half Ainu. He hid it of course, but not from me. People often hide nothing from me. Akira Gengei belonged to the last generation that spoke the language well. Everywhere in Hokkaido, at the time, Ainu parents raised their children in ignorance. They thought that the best way to protect them from others' scorn was to conceal from them their origins. They thought that the suffering of their race would disappear along with the shame of belonging to that race. They were not afraid of dying out in the process, because they believed that a people is still itself, no matter what name it assumes. Gengei-san explained to me that a more accurate translation of *Shiretoko* would have been "there where the world goes beyond itself," or "there where the world bursts its banks." That pleased me enormously. We were not, in Rausu, at the outer limits of everything, but already on the other side.

I came from the ends of the earth with pebbles in my pockets.

They may have told you. They couldn't have told you why. No one ever knew. Other than Reiko. I brought them to sow, like seeds, and carry with me a bit of my native landscape. You can plant pebbles where you like and nothing of them will sprout, nothing of them will grow, and that's perhaps a sad notion for people here and elsewhere, but not for me. I spread them on the road one night, among pebbles just like themselves. The pebbles, like the landscapes, were the same. There was nothing of myself to bring here, and I didn't come for that. I was far away now, where no one could ever find me, but I soon realized that I'd chosen the identical land, that I had always been, as here, remote from the world, and there would be no elsewhere, never an elsewhere, until I transcended myself.

The village was called Rausu, but the elders still called it Uembetsu, because it had for a long time borne that name. The summers were mild here and the village full of visitors, but the winters were terrible, just like where I'd come from, for months they cut off all of Hokkaido's north coast from the world. That's when I most liked the life here. There were the same long mountains everywhere, a bit soft, a bit lazy, that stretched out low in the landscape as far as the eye could see, and the trees were like at home, I won't say where, black silhouettes that kept their needles for the whole year, and held the snow in their branches until they were like great soft ghosts frozen into the winter.

Reiko says:

It's my uncle who took care of me after the boat carrying my parents sank to the bottom of the sea of Okhotsk. He was already looking after me before that, and as a little girl I felt as if my father, my mother and myself were dolls with porcelain faces on exhibit at the Inoué property, curios gathering dust while waiting for my uncle's visits. My mother dusted and sewed. My father drank, in the village and at home, but was always able to eat with us in silence and to climb stiff-backed up to his room. When my uncle arrived, my parents became servants and I became the lady of the manor. Rausu was the summer estate of my uncle Inoué. He was the master and father and the unofficial mayor of the village, and he never came in the winter and it seemed that we ourselves in the winter didn't really exist.

My uncle spent part of the summer with me, the little orphan. When cold began to creep into the air, he had the idea of finding this woman, Misaka, and asking her to be my governess. My uncle was rich. He did business in Sapporo. He had enough money to pay a governess for me, and enough money so that all I wore was silk. When I was small he said that I was the flower of Nemuro, the sub-prefecture, and that now I was the flower of Hokkaido, and when he spoke to me about this woman, he told me that with her lessons I would be both a true Japanese and a real American, that I could be the most beautiful woman on earth, both the flower of the Empire and of the entire world. When that became so, I would go to live with him in the capital and perhaps, one day, we would visit Paris, London and New York together.

She was a strange woman, Misaka. Tall. With red hair and green eyes. I'd never seen a woman like that, not in Rausu, but I recognized her right away. In front of my uncle she talked to me as to a little girl. She stroked my hair and I looked right into her eyes and I knew that deep down this woman didn't like children. I saw that she'd never wanted life inside of her, but that she would have wanted me inside her, and that she wanted me for herself. So I played the flower of Hokkaido. I threw myself into her arms, smiling and hugging her tight. My uncle also smiled.

"I told you she'd love you, Misaka-sensei."

Oh, you have every right to call me a liar and tell me I couldn't feel that way when I was eleven. As for me, I have the right to stick out my tongue at you and tell you that you're the liars, you're the dogs.

2

Misaka says:

I can tell you how it all began.

I found her one morning, on her bed, naked from waist to feet, her thin legs and pink sex settled on the covers. She was in the midst of cutting a deep gash in the flesh of her right thigh with a tracing wheel. There was blood on the sheets, blood on her fingers, and blood at the corners of her lips. For that instant, for that instant only, I will be judged. I could have run to her and taken her in my arms and asked her why she was doing what she was doing, and told her it must end, told her I'd help her to stop, that I knew how to make her stop.

Instead, when she raised her eyes to me, when she asked me, "Is it bad, what I'm doing, Misaka?" I threw myself on her but I didn't stop her. I told her that whoever wants to do that has the right to do it, and I told her she must never feel guilty nor be ashamed nor ever think that in punishing her body she was damaging someone else's property. I embraced her, I enfolded her in my arms, and I let her bleed onto my clothes before disinfecting her wound and dressing it with gauze. After, I stood up before her, I slowly took off my clothes, and I showed her, among the scars left on my body by my wanderings and by men, the marks of all those wounds I'd inflicted on myself.

Reiko says:

Misaka was my father, my mother, my governess, my mistress, my doomed soul, and my initiator. That was no news to anyone, but what I want to say is that she was also, often, like my little girl, like a child who trembled and sobbed in my arms, because where pain was concerned I was better than her, in pain I was greater than her.

In the beginning, Misaka didn't even know what *jigai* meant.

I'm the one who told her that spouses once committed ritual suicide by cutting the jugular vein, seated, legs tucked under their buttocks. Enemy soldiers found the villages they invaded emptied of all life, houses deserted, furnished only with low tables and dead women, upright and noble, their ankles bound tightly so that no soldier might be tempted to wrest from their dead bodies what, living, they could have taken from them by force. I'm the one who decided that together we would honour no tradition. It was I who resolved that we would not mutilate ourselves to deny ourselves to all, but to offer ourselves to each other. We would mutilate ourselves without dying, without ceremony, our legs spread wide.

Oh, you have every right to say it's all false, that I couldn't know all that, and that I ought not to be there to tell my story because I'm dead. As for me, I've every right to tell you that it's you who knows nothing, you who are aware of nothing.

The men say:

We have a good idea of what happened down there, all that time, and we all know how it ended, but no one knows how it began. At first we didn't notice anything. Reiko's prolonged absence from among the children eventually caught the attention of the wives. It also became clear that Misaka-sensei and the little Inoué had not left the property for more than a year. Some men who had arrived at dawn one day sometimes opened the gates and came to buy provisions for them in the village.

While we were wondering, sitting at Akira Gengei's one noon-hour, whether we ought to send someone to check things out, a child came in and said:

"Come see."

Two women were crossing the village, limping, one supporting the other, swathed in large purple capes, their faces masked by hoods. They walked to the stream, then went back to the property without saying anything to anyone. The frightened children said that when they passed in front of them they saw their faces from underneath, and swore that they had no more noses nor lips nor eyelids, and that their faces were like those of yūrei, like those of the dead. We would have liked to contradict them, but we'd all noticed that only three naked feet protruded from under their capes, and that on each, several toes had been chiselled off.

3

The men say:

There was already nothing that could be done to protect them from themselves and the madness that had seized hold of their minds. During their progress they were surrounded by two bands of five bodyguards that they had chosen and paid, as we later learned, with money belonging to Sapporo's uncle. The first was from here, the second were *gaijin*.

The first were bad men, consumed with a dark nostalgia for the licence their ancestors enjoyed under the ancient shogunates. The second were not much better. The Great War had horrified the entire world. These men had built their nests and grown to maturity there less like birds of prey than like reptiles, whose pale eyes and chill blood they shared. In their barracks they had been told, "You'll see, when you have to kill a Boche with no bullets in your gun, you'll see, when you throw yourself on him screaming over his screams and stick your bayonet in his gut not knowing if he's found a way to thrust his into yours, and you watch his gaze go dim not knowing if you're guttering out as well, then you'll see what that does to you." They went off, they saw what there was to see, they didn't die, and they felt nothing. Not fear, not disgust, not pleasure, not anything. Their comrades in the regiment had gone back to their villages where they tried not to think of the war, tried to hide their mangled or absent limbs in the sleeves of their shirts and their pant legs, tried to forget the great swathes of their souls that had collapsed within them and now surfaced only in nocturnal outbursts of terror loosed from the depths of a nightmare. Meanwhile the soldiers of fortune roamed the world and reaped the benefits of this monstrous void in themselves as though it were a gift.

The children trained their narrowed eyes through the cracks in the palisade and reported that these men were abandoning themselves to barbaric jousts, taking turns doing tricks like little kittens, some learning to wield the katana, and others to action the breech of the assault rifles, all fighting bare-handed under the afternoon sun, and sometimes, haloed by lanterns, into the night, to the immense delight of Misaka and Reiko, who were much entertained by these games, and applauded them wildly from the veranda with their bound hands.

We wrote a letter to the uncle in Sapporo to inform him of the situation. He arrived in a car, had the doors to his own house thrown open with great difficulty, and came out a half-hour later, white-faced and hollow-eyed. He spoke with the mayor, told him that he was cutting off support for Reiko, that that was all he could do, and that with a bit of luck the renegades would disappear when they ran out of money.

"Do you want to be informed when that happens?" asked the mayor.

The uncle from Sapporo got into his car and said that we would have to exercise our own good judgment and deal with his niece and his other possessions in the village as we thought best, because he would never return to Rausu, and would never open a letter sent from here.

We realized too late that the renegades had found more in Rausu than a good income. After a few months, as we awaited their imminent departure, the mercenaries began to descend on the town every week to extort money from the businessmen and citizens and bring back supplies to their new mistresses.

Reiko says:

I breathed deeply so my uncle would hear the whistling Misaka and I made since we'd slashed away our lips, the sucking noise every breath required to return to our mouths the naked drool flowing onto our gums. I breathed like that for a long moment, then, in one flourish, I spread the wings of my cape while lifting my arms as though to fly away. I wanted him to see below, where I was unclad. I wanted him to see all the marks, the old ones that wouldn't have had time to heal even if I'd lived a thousand years, and the new ones, unsettling, hideous, because Misaka and I always waited a day or two before disinfecting the wounds, to feel the pus clinging claw-like to our flesh, like an animal holding to its lair. I wanted him to see that I could not promenade on his arm in a ball dress in Rio or New York, nor sunbathe in Monte Carlo. I wanted him to see my flat, blank breast that would never suckle a child. I wanted him to know that Misaka and I had together determined the definitive length and form of my cleft.

Oh, you may believe if you like that I had no say in all that, and that all the dissipation you find so horrible was forced on me by Misaka, but you will not talk about it because on this subject you never dare speak a word, and there is nothing that has been forced into my mouth, into my cleft, between my buttocks or into my flesh that I have despised as much as your silence, that silence sour as milk that Misaka the accursed never made me drink.

4

Reiko says:

I did not invent the art; the art invented itself through me. In due course we became aware that certain wounds, as they healed, imprinted on the flesh sinuosities that resembled writing. Because I had a finer hand, Misaka wanted me to tattoo characters on our skin with a knife blade, but I said that would be too easy, too obvious, and I didn't want their symbols on her skin or mine. I said that, in any case, what made these marks interesting was not the script, nor even the movement it sometimes suggested, but the thickness, the texture. I knew our path was not to draw, whether it be with a razor, on the skin itself, but to shape the flesh. I began by experimenting on myself, finding a way to open up the tissues and have them hold in the desired position, preventing the wounds from closing over and the skin from drying out, blending in alcohol, tincture of iodine, and wood varnish. Soon the forms became too complex for me to produce them on my own body, and I began to carve into Misaka's flesh. The art gradually became a blend of engraving, sculpture, and fabric design. I dug furrows and cut strips of skin with dressmaking shears, gouges, and burrs; I kneaded the oozing flesh with my hands and shored it up with cross-stitching and satin stitching; I inserted rivets, splints, and pins between the strips when my configurations required open skin and erect parings.

The problem was that I was both more skilled than Misaka, and had greater endurance. The art was very hard on her. She sweated, vomited, and fainted. We had to experiment with drugs, but often the pain became too severe to be dulled even by powerful opiates.

Curiously, it was the men who found the solution when they sent us one of their spouses to renew the contact between us. The renegades brought us Azumi in the middle of the afternoon, on a Thursday. She had made herself lovely in her summer dress, and had arrived with gifts. We talked to her about art. We showed her the results, on Misaka's body. We saw the curiosity that lent a gleam to her large black pupils. Misaka bared her shoulder, we had her drink a soothing infusion, and I placed myself beside her with my instruments. She was breathing deeply. I sought Misaka's eyes and saw that she'd already understood. We'd been missing one ingredient. You needed to be three to practise the art. Misaka went down on all fours and only a few seconds after I'd set to work, thrust her face between the legs of Azumi, already dazed by the drug and the pain. Azumi didn't protest, she even unfastened her dress a bit more and in a sudden spasm, offered her cleft to Misaka's mouth.

I bested her in suffering, but with her tongue she was superior to me.

We let Azumi leave for home later, dazed, dishevelled, and covered in her own blood. Misaka well knew that we'd gone too far. Immediately afterwards, she said to the renegades:

"Get ready. The villagers will be on their way."

But there was no attack that night. Instead, Azumi returned the next day with a young wife even prettier than herself, who pointed with her finger to the motif, much resembling a gillyflower, which I'd carved into her friend's soft shoulder, and said:

"I want one, too."

I called forth a wood spider, with her right breast as the abdomen, and drew its fine sparassid legs from her bosom's thin flesh. Meanwhile Misaka thrust her face between her legs, and Azumi, without anyone having to say anything, went down on her knees behind Misaka and dipped two fingers, soon dripping wet, into her cleft.

In no time at all, women were arriving from the village and the entire peninsula, to be sculpted. This beauty Misaka and I had invented was now walking the streets, given prominence by the spouses' strategically perforated dresses, and the dismayed ugliness of the husbands.

Oh, you have every right to turn the page and declare that it's all a bad dream in which Misaka and I drift about like shadows behind curtains. But I have the right to defy you, to tell you to lift the bedclothes in the dawn hours, to accustom your eyes to the half-light without waking your loved one, and to swear to me that you know the meaning of every tattoo on her body, and the origin of every burn.

The men say:

We made an enormous mistake by sending Mabuto's wife to the Inoué domain, and the horror that ensued was immeasurable. The repugnant mutilations that Misaka and Reiko inflicted on flesh became a fashion, an uncontainable compulsion, an enchantment, and there was no way to break the spell, not in reasoning with the wives, or in crying after them, or in trying to shake them out of their torpor, or by beating them. We were at least able to make them talk, but their accounts were all the more shocking in that we knew each one was keeping many details to herself.

They said that Misaka and Reiko were lovers. That they embraced by touching their foreheads together, merging their lidless gazes, and licking, each in turn, the other's gums and teeth. They said that Misaka ate glass. That she crushed electric light bulbs, which she had brought from the mainland, in her hands, and swallowed them one by one, like candies, the splinters stained with blood. She mixed them with flower petals and shari rice. Later, there flowed from between her legs a rose-coloured liquid she offered to the women like a serving for a meal, one they said was as delicate as the raw flesh of a fish. They also said that withered and solitary women come from nowhere asked for their bodies to be entirely sculpted, and that the renegades had buried their martyred remains behind the property, below the hills.

We would have wanted to treat these stories as simple tales, and we would doubtless have succeeded in doing so, if these mutilated wives, sometimes amputated and blinded, had not strolled through the village streets in greater and greater numbers to display their wounds like brand new silk kimonos.

Misaka says:

According to the renegades, the men complained that from beyond the palisade there reached their ears cries of desolation and death. Say what they liked, the men indeed heard guttural sounds of an alien nature, rollicking belly to belly with the cries of pain that issued from the villa. Something was cavorting in company with the pain, mating with it inside the shared cries, something that, being so intimate with pain, showed itself to be even more shocking. The men knew perfectly well what it was, but they had no name for it, and even if they'd had one, they would under no circumstances have pronounced it.

They did have one, however, to designate the demons of Christian lands, and they set themselves to covering the Inoué property's walls with red paint:

悪魔

When the renegades told me about it and asked me what they should do, I told them to leave the ideograms where they were on the palisade, and to call me from now on by my chosen name, Akuma.

5

Once, once only, Misaka says:

Long before this day, the last day, I took Reiko in my arms, as in the beginning, when she was only a child. I embraced her, and afterwards I said:

"My love, the flesh that grows over what is cut is new flesh. Perhaps for this reason, precisely, something awaits us at the end of art that is not death. Perhaps our work is a work of life, perhaps when our bodies will be nothing but open wounds we will be reborn anew, like two twin sisters. Perhaps in the end a million scars will leave our skin as smooth as that of a newborn."

Reiko looked at me with sadness, and replied:

"You're wrong, Misaka. You're as wrong as you can be. None of us is born without scars. We are created by the meeting of flesh and flesh, we are the fruit of one only, but we remain coiled like a voracious tumour in her belly, until we are torn from her breast and the thread is cut that binds us to her. There will be no return to the beginning, beautiful sensei. We are brought into this world by the steel of a blade, Misaka, and you and I are born each day a bit more."

One last time, Reiko says:

I never mutilated my tongue. Pleasure without pain is just a masquerade, but we must keep intact those parts that can give pleasure, because without it pain is only pain. You can cut off your fingers with big pruning shears, but you have to conserve at least one to penetrate the cunt up to the womb, you can amputate one foot with a hacksaw, but you have to keep the other to press it against the loved one's cleft when your hands are otherwise engaged, you can lop off toes with a chisel, but you have to keep at least one stump to suck, you can rip off eyelids, make holes in lips, and slice off earlobes, but you always have to take care of your tongue, to treat well the only tongue you own, as it's precious and doesn't easily heal.

Without it, you wouldn't be able to say that I'm lying, that two women would never do all that we've done, and that we are only paper ghosts, unable to suffer or bleed. Without it, I could turn my back on you as I am doing now, and go silent as I soon will, but I would not have been able to accomplish, on this next to last day, the one thing I'd refused myself up to that point.

On the night before the last day, in the darkness, over the muffled laughter of the renegades playing cards on the floor above, I told Misaka that I loved her.

In the end, the men say:

We'd screwed up our courage for a whole year, we'd saved up and armed ourselves with guns bought on the mainland, with rusted blades and clubs. We knew they wouldn't prevail against the renegades, but we counted on our numbers and on our conviction that deep within themselves, the ronins and the *gaijins* must also have felt that this madness had to end. Even the wives no longer visited the Inoué property. Because we'd ordered them not to, of course, because they almost all had their own sculptures now, it was true, but also, and we knew it even if they refused to admit it, because they were afraid of Akuma and Reiko. They had seen things there about which they did not want to speak, they'd known women who had chosen to remain with the mistresses and who had never emerged from the property, they'd understood that all that was but horror, and they had returned to their duties and to reason. The children could bear witness to those horrors, those who had seen the graves dug below the property.

We crossed the village in a large pack, our lights troubling the darkness, battered the gate open with a sledgehammer and crowbars, and began to scale the slope leading to the house. At first we thought it was aflame. A pyre was burning in front of it, a gigantic bonfire loosing into the night air a stench of grease, wood, and solvent, and beyond which our eyes, dazzled, could not make out the structure of a house intact. We thought at first that the house itself was burning, and we saw ten black silhouettes loom up between us and the flames. We all felt a frigid chill run up our spines, we loaded our guns, unsheathed our blades, and closed our fingers around our staffs, tight enough to crack our joints. The renegades' silhouettes shrank the more they drew away from the fire and came near to us, but their giant shadows danced with the flames and stretched out across the ground as far as the soles of our shoes.

Someone, bellowing, launched himself at the first of the renegades, his arms raised over his head to deal a heavy blow with his bludgeon. He'd hardly had time to begin his movement when the ronin took two steps forward and held the tip of his sabre to the man's pulsing throat. He didn't kill him.

He made a sign for him to step aside, he ordered us all to step aside, then without a glance, plunged into the corridor that had been opened up, with the rest of the damned following behind.

The last one stopped and said:

"It's over. You shouldn't go up there."

You had to be stupid to think we'd not go to see, to be certain that the threat was no more. Most of us rushed to the house, skirting the bonfire, and only a few turned back along with the renegades.

A strong wind rose up later that night, and blew embers and fiery brands into the house, through the windows. It was burned to its foundations, razed to the ground. No one ever missed it, but all of us who'd climbed on up, hours before the fire had been declared, regretted not having taken the renegade's advice.

15

Akira Gengei said to himself, in Ainu:

The two women are now silent. The men here never speak of them, and on their orders, neither do their wives. And yet I feel, I sense that some of them still tend to their wounds, care for them and reopen them to keep Reiko's art alive. Perhaps I'm the only one here who can still speak of all that, because I live in a language that no one any more understands.

The men who scaled the hill towards the house, despite the renegades' warnings, found Misaka and Reiko carved up, dismembered, hacked into pieces that were scattered to all four corners of the house. The men must have been gratified, they must have told themselves that at last they had received their punishment, but they couldn't really know if what they saw before their eyes was punishment or rapture. They couldn't be certain. A fissure had worked its way into their minds, like a razor blade through the delicate flesh of their wives. They would have liked to believe that an ogre had staved in the doors of the property to bear off the women and drag them by their hair down to hell, but they had the vague feeling that whatever had come in search of Misaka and Reiko possessed the attributes of a woman and the attributes of a man, and that its fury had blown upon them like the wind through the window, making no more noise than the pad of a cat in an unmade bed. They knew that past a certain point, nothing had happened to Misaka and Reiko that they had not desired, and that whatever demon had come to ravish them, they had invoked it themselves, they had brought down its hands and claws upon themselves.

The house's cold ashes were strewn over the peninsula, and the property is still abandoned. Travellers expected at Rausu never arrive, and the news of their disappearance reaches us by letter from Honshu, which is also an island, but that the people of Hokkaido still call "the mainland."

As of the first snows, we find in places where no one ever sends flocks to graze, hoof prints, those of a buffalo or a goat walking on two legs. An old man told me one night that deeper still into the forest, there in the midst of brambles and thorns, where the bears themselves clear no paths, another series of prints joins up with those of the goat. They never run side by side for long, as if their owners knew each other well enough to exchange a greeting, but not enough to walk in convoy. Those prints are indistinct, like a child's boot with at the tip a few red, almost brown drops like blood in the snow. The prints make three baby steps and fifteen drops of blood, three baby steps and fifteen drops of blood, three baby steps and fifteen drops of blood.

Paris in the Rain
BLOOD SISTERS III

HE'D DIED deep in the woods and they'd taken him to the funeral parlour to try and deal with the damage. He'd worked for Abitibi Consolidated, which everyone around called the Console. None of the guys had seen what happened. He'd been split open from shoulder to hip by a machine that could trim trees tall as cathedrals. No one knew how he'd got in the way of the lopper. They were deep in the woods and the guys said that the day before there was a little snow. In June, mind you. Seems he'd made a stain on the ground as big as a puddle of water, thick as molasses and red as a harlot's mouth.

She was there just by chance. A friend had found her work in his parents' bistro in France. She'd be staying ten days in Paris before getting on a train for Brittany, and she'd come to say goodbye to her parents before taking off.

The woman at the funeral parlour had been brought up to date, and she met her in a room that reminded her of the reading room in her grandparents' house. The woman had very beautiful hands, with small fingers, both plump and delicate, and that's all she could bring herself to think about.

"I'm sorry that you can't attend the funeral."

"Thank you."

"You're part of the family?"

"Yes."

"His daughter?"

"No."

There was a silence.

"You're going back to Montreal tomorrow?"

"Yes. I'm taking the plane for Paris on Thursday."

The woman sighed.

"I've never been to Paris."

"Neither have I."

Something wasn't quite right, and the woman wouldn't understand what it was until two days later. Sitting in front of the television set beside her sleeping husband, she would think again of the young woman and her heady odour and her large breasts offered to view through her dress's plunging neckline. The colour black was the only thing appropriate in her appearance. The cut of her clothes and her perfume and her hair and her thick red lipstick and the brightness of her eyes spoke of something forbidden in that place. The woman would think of the young woman and then those deadly beauties in crime novels who poison their husbands to get their hands on the insurance money.

"She looked like a black widow."

This idea, expressed aloud to herself alone, raised a thousand questions, and at that moment the only person capable of answering them was flying thirty thousand feet above the Atlantic.

The embalmer was standing right beside his table when the widow entered the room. He turned to face her, and said:

"My sympathies, Miss."

She didn't answer.

He'd prepared a speech to warn her. Either he delivered it badly or she didn't listen or there was no way to make her change her mind, because she said:

"I want to see him."

The embalmer sighed. He took the sheet by the hem and folded it back to bare the cadaver to halfway down the chest. The woman didn't move, not a gesture, not a twitch.

"I want to be with him for a while."

"You'll be all right?"

"Yes."

She stayed there alone, beside the corpse.

It didn't even look like a cadaver any more. You could imagine it was a body by the curve of the neck and left shoulder. The same line was interrupted on the right. The same line was broken off, splintered, and twisted on the right. The rest was a sculpture fashioned from an open wound with mutilated flesh and strips of grey skin bruised yellow and black.

Facing the carcass, she took from her handbag a sheet of paper folded in four. She opened it with care. The sheet was covered in tiny red handwriting. She cleared her throat and refolded it and began to talk while holding it, damp, in the palm of her hand.

"I came to tell you that I'm glad you're dead. I know you didn't only do bad things in your life, but I'm happy all the same and never never will I feel guilty for that. When I was small, during the catechism, Madame Verreault talked to us about the good Lord who was the father of little Jesus and who pardoned all our transgressions and forgave us all our sins. Grandmother had a bible. Thicker than the New Testament they gave us at school. Inside there were stories of the time before Jesus, and in those stories God doesn't look like Father Christmas. Whenever he feels like it he imposes bizarre taboos, and he's appalled by just about everything men do. He asks them to bathe their sins in blood, and to cut off the hands of thieves and to stone unfaithful women. I asked Madame Verreault how those two gods could inhabit the same book, and who'd decided to pass them off as only one. The catechism doesn't have ready-made answers for questions like that. She did her best. She said God had always wanted to make peace in the world, and for that he had for a long time to present himself as very hard in order to hold in check all the evil running rampant in the hearts of men. God had pretended to be terrible before sending his Son to reveal to us that he was love. For our own good. A bit like my parents who loved me had to punish me when I was naughty. It was a nice try but I was already smart enough to recognize an explanation that was too convenient. I kept that in mind for a long time, and years later I finally understood. Because of you. It wasn't the first time that you came to me but it was the first time that you said you loved me. That's when I understood. God loved you like he loved me. He loved us both, He loved us, strange bed mates, you the burly man and me the child, he loved your hands on me and your sweaty underclothes, he loved my cold feet and my icy nose, he loved your past suffering as much as mine in the future. That's when I understood, I'm telling you. God is love and that's why he's terrible. You can't live, knowing that. You can just destroy your life and destroy your body and push others away and hurt others. You can just be evil and I was evil all the time and it's your fault and the fault of the stupid God who loved you like he loved me, of God who loved you, big dirty dog, and who loved me, damaged little girl. Today I'm fine. I know that a God listens to murderous prayers, and I know that stretched out beside me you were an abomination to him. I've come to tell you that it doesn't bother me if God divided your soul in two to bring the good half close to him. It doesn't bother me if God was with you while the lopper tore you in two because now that you look like that, I forgive you too."

The widow applied a humid kiss to the brow half torn from the dead man, and wiped from the corners of her eyes tears that were not there, and left the embalming room and the funeral home and slept at her parents' and took the bus to Montreal where she arrived with the smell of cadavers still stuck in her nostrils and on her palate. She knew that smell. She'd smelled it often when she'd helped her great-uncle to dig graves in the village cemetery. Sometimes he dug a grave to bury a woman on top of her husband, and he was afraid at each blow of the shovel of breaking through the coffin's rotten wood. The earth around them reeked of decomposition and at night she brought back to the house an odour of death that her sisters came to sniff, clotted in her hair, and that only disappeared after long, scalding baths.

Later she worked in restaurant kitchens and brought home with her odours of raw meat and cooking with spices and garlic, which never really disappeared, but at least they were the odours of life, and Paul said, laughing, that he felt like he was making love to a braised lamb. He was working at the university library. She would have liked to smell on his skin the fresh aroma of books they bought at bookstores or the rank odour of the books they unearthed in second-hand stores, but books don't leave the same traces on people, and she never found any scent on him of paper, old or new.

It was Paul who came to drive her to the airport on Thursday.

They stayed in the car, watching the drops of rain slip like snails down the windshield. At a certain point she asked:

"What's going to happen with us?"

Paul held her hand for a long time, staring ahead of him. She knew he wouldn't kiss her.

"We'll talk about it when you get back."

"Maybe I won't come back."

He pretended to look for something in his jacket pockets.

"Come. We'll unload your suitcases."

The widow drank three Perriers on the plane, thinking about her ragged twenties. For years she'd stalked, unthinking, the lights over the doors of bars that invited you in like little birds befogged by mountain ash berries, who throw themselves against their own reflections in the windows. After, there'd been Paul, and all those years she'd loved him to the point of nausea, of not being able to sleep at night. She worked at the time in a rather tough neighbourhood. Getting off at two in the morning, she'd call Paul from the bistro so he'd come to meet her. They'd spot each other from a distance in winter in the middle of snowstorms, and for some hundreds of metres they'd appear and disappear from each other's sight in great clouds of drifting snow that they themselves stirred up. They kissed and went home and rid their bones of cold by rubbing numb limbs together, while their bodies embraced the warmth and the skin of the other. You had to be very poor and desperate to love each other like that, and there was some comfort in knowing she'd never go back there. She had no trouble now paying her bills, and the great adolescent ache had dulled within her. She was safe now forever from turmoil, but was paying the price.

There is no true love for those who take cover from the storm.

Through the airplane window she observed the clouds, which didn't look at all the same on high as they did from down below. From underneath they were all curves, and formed sheep or hills or faces. But from aloft they were broken lines, and formed arches and streets and facades and for a moment she thought to herself that things would have been different with Paul if they'd been able to live in one of those cities in the clouds. Soon Ireland's pasturelands appeared in the window, and as far as Orly she watched Europe unfold as a life-size map, and thought no more of anything.

In Paris, jet-lagged, she took possession of the apartment she'd rented for the week. It was two rooms, furnished with a kitchenette, bathroom, and flowered balcony, on an upper floor of an Eleventh Arrondissement high-rise. In the afternoon she went up Avenue Philippe-Auguste and the Boulevard de Ménilmontant to Père Lachaise. She bestowed a sloppy kiss on Oscar Wilde's monument, paused for a long time before Édith Piaf's, and meditated over the remains, minus his heart, of Frédéric Chopin. The next day she visited Notre-Dame and saw two lovers light a candle, wondering what they might be pledging to each other. She then walked along the Seine, crossed Pont Royal, and stopped at the Musée d'Orsay, where she lingered over the *Déjeuner sur l'herbe* to examine the curves of this young woman who Paul had often claimed looked a lot like her.

She ate alone and went back to the apartment, heavy-hearted. She felt like crying, and had trouble breathing. She'd suffocated as a young girl in her village, she'd suffocated as a young woman in Montreal, and she suffocated now as a merry widow in the world's capital. She went to bed with the growing unease that sometimes stopped her from leaving the house in the morning, and even from dragging herself out from beneath the bedclothes.

She was awakened at dawn by thunder. When she got out of bed, she saw through the window that the city was wrapped in fog and covered by an opaque layer of grey clouds. Later on, sirens wailed in the midst of the storm to signal that it was noon. The sirens dated from the war, and could have been those heralding an invasion. The rain pounded down on the city like shrapnel, and the widow watched it falling all day long from the balcony.

She saw the Eiffel Tower's steel structure dissolve into an anthracite silhouette, then vanish completely. She saw the rain swallow up the Panthéon, the Montparnasse tower, and Notre-Dame. She saw the Butte Montmartre and Sacré-Coeur being washed away like dead trees in a rushing river.

She thought: terrible dreams are coming true.

The Romans and the barbarians wanted to destroy Paris, the English toyed with the idea for a hundred years, and Hitler wished for it with all his dark soul, not suspecting that the man responsible for razing the city would show himself more loyal to the splendours of Lutetia than to all the swastikas in Berlin.

For millennia, they had failed.

For two hours the widow hovered between sky and earth and watched the rain wipe away Paris.

The next day she got up, took a shower, and went down to the tobacconist to buy blonde Gitanes and a *café crème*. It was hot. Nothing remained of the storm, other than the heavy humidity being exhaled by the paving stones. She went back home to change and met an old man in the elevator who lived on the same floor. They greeted each other. He was a polite gentleman who wore a thick corduroy jacket and large, tortoiseshell glasses. He ought to have had a pile of books under his arm, but he was carrying records, old 33 r.p.m. jazz recordings. Dexter Gordon, Miles Davis, Sonny Rollins.

"Are you renting the Becqueret apartment?"

"No," she replied, "I live here."

"Really? You're moving in?"

She smiled.

"I've always lived here."

The old man looked at her, perplexed, then he smiled in turn.

"It's true, you're right."

The elevator door opened. The old man added:

"And if you'll allow me, Mademoiselle: in all this time, you've always been right."

Returning home after an aperitif with friends a few days later, the widow came across a writer, much prized by the media, sitting at a table with a young woman, in front of a half-empty plate. She stared at him through the glass as if she were looking at a screen, not realizing what she was doing, until he lifted his head and gazed back at her with annoyance.

She gave a start, burst out laughing, and strode off. That was the most enduring impression the city left on her. Paris was a large zoo where intellectuals were shut up behind café windows.

It was time now to make her way north.

The Centre of Leisure and Forgetfulness
ARVIDA II

MY GRANDMOTHER, mother of my father, often said:

"There are no thieves in Arvida."

The Americans built the town beside the aluminum smelter in a hundred and thirty-five days. There'd been nothing around for 200 million years, then there was the Alcan smelter, and a hundred and thirty-five days later, a town. The spiteful claimed that only after the 1941 strike did the Americans decide to no longer treat the workers like cattle, but my father and others said that was a lie.

Look at the evidence.

The Americans allowed the four parishes to be built around enormous churches, and contented themselves with two chapels, one Evangelical and the other Anglican, two little chapels in red brick, one beside the other, in front of the Notre-Dame-du-Sourire school, and beside Riverside School on Boulevard des Saguenéens. The sinuous and labyrinthine designs of the town's streets, the proximity of the bosses' houses to those of the foremen and workers, the big parks at each corner, and the flanking of the houses of worship by two schools and a skating rink, everything in Arvida attested to the fact that this model town was the little utopia of a billionaire philanthropist, built from scratch right in the middle of nowhere. The plan was laid out in full knowledge that the sons of the bosses would be playing hockey and baseball with the offspring of the others, that the daughters of the one would be doing their homework alongside those of the others, and that all of them, boys and girls, would perhaps one day be sleeping in the same bed.[2]

That's how the town was seen in my family, and even today it's hard to budge my father. In 2004 there was a television report to mark some anniversary or other, and it was suggested that the original parish of Sainte-Thérèse be declared a UNESCO heritage site. There was old Madame Tretiak, wife of a worker, who claimed that in the little house where she lived with her husband and eight children, the Alcan builders had skimped on the insulation. She said that in the depths of winter the walls were covered in a thick layer of ice. When one of my visiting friends repeated the story, my father dismissed his argument with the back of his hand.

"The walls of the house froze because it was the good woman Tretiak who was skimping on the heating. I'll bet you a twenty that she herself ripped the insulation out of the walls to add it to the lining in her coats. She was tight with everything, Madame Tretiak. Her husband drank almost all his pay plus half that of his teetotalling brother. He left her two bucks a week for the laundry, the groceries, and the bills, and she still put something aside for a rainy day."

It was Arthur Vining Davis's dream, and he christened it with an acronym drawn from the first two letters of his own three names. Andrew Mellon, the richest man in the world, financed the construction. There were men who designed it and others who built it, and the employees of Alcoa and Alcan have lived there ever since.

---

2   It has to be said, however, that there's something a bit overblown in this picture. In the city's original plan, before the parishes were founded and the lots fully occupied, the "English" town and the "workers'" town were built a good distance from each other.

From time to time there is talk of its possible consecration as a UNESCO heritage site. I think that began even as it was being built, and it's become a running gag between my father and me. Whenever we pass an Arvidian house to which the years have not been kind, a duplex whose owners have painted their halves in different colours, or a lawn indifferently tended, one of us says:

"Now that one, it'd be best not to show it to the guys from UNESCO."

It all started up again in 2010. In an interview, the municipal counsellor Carl Dufour declared:

"Without Arvida, the Germans might have won the war."

A grotesque claim with one merit: that of being the most outrageous exaggeration in the history of a town that had all the same witnessed the birth of my father. It's true that almost all the aluminum that went into the fuselage of allied planes was produced at the Vaudreuil factory. The installations were protected during most of the war by anti-aircraft batteries that formed strange totems on the grass around the buildings. Of course, Arvida was not Pearl Harbor, nor London, nor even Dresden. The Japanese and the Germans had plenty to keep them busy on the Russian steppes or in the great Pacific powder keg without coming over to disturb the uneasy calm of the population of Arvida.[3]

I understand, of course, what Councillor Dufour was trying to say, but it seems to me that in wanting to revive the town's obscure historical importance, he seriously misrepresented its nature.

Arvida has never been a town at the crux of history, but rather a place resolutely outside it. There were no thieves in

---

3 Another Arvidian myth may be similarly discredited: for a long time it was bruited about that the original design for the town had been conceived with the idea of tracing on its very ground the letters A-R-V-I-D-A, visible from the sky. Such a project, which would imply inscribing a bit of the world's map onto the world itself, would have been unthinkable in the watchful minds of urbanists between the wars.

Arvida, at least not many, but there were, drawn by the wealth to be found there or sought out by its laboratories, Americans, Englishmen, and people from the four corners of the earth.

From Russia came the Marinoffs, one of whose daughters, Sonia, is my godmother.

From Italy came the machinist Dan Belladonne, Brian Santoni of the employment office, the restaurant owner Amato Verdone, and old man Zampieri, who laid down marble and terrazzo, and who was the grandfather of the Bourque brothers.

From Poland came Matt Barkovitz, the mechanic Joe Pollock, and my grandparents' neighbour, Mister Belinak.

From Holland had come the chemist Neil Van Dalen.

From Greece came Gus Tectonidis, and the friend of the family Vic Kostopoulos.

From Japan came Frank Watanabe, the engineer. It appears he was not alone: a photo from between the wars shows the former factory pay office, a shed that looked like a train station out of an old Western, with in front of it, swaying in the breeze and suspended from two chains, a sign with the words PAY OFFICE written in French, English, and in Japanese characters.

From Catalonia came Jordi Bonet, just long enough to create a large mural on the front of the city hall.

From the pasturelands of Ireland and the heaths of Scotland came, try to sort them out: the other Archibald family, the Burrows, Terry Loucks, Neil Balcon, Reidy Smith of the Arvida orchestra, the Duffys, the O'Dorthys and the Fountains, Teddy Hallahan, Stephen Lee (Peter Lee's father), the expert carpenter Médéric McLaughlin, father of Popeye McLaughlin and fourteen other children who looked as alike as two drops of water.

I've forgotten some, obviously. All these people had come to Arvida, drawn to a Nordic version of El Dorado, an

American Dream that had veered some thousands of kilometres off course. They'd often come to forget things, and never, never ever, to remember anything. Certainly not a war.

Another paternal story of larceny illustrates this principle in catastrophic fashion. My grandfather, a foreman in the painting workshop, was responsible for purchases, and sometimes received a visit from Mister Addams, who dealt in products to be used in industrial renovation. Mister Addams was a tall, strapping Welshman, blond and blue-eyed, good looking but with equine teeth. He'd arrive with an armful of alcohol, cheap gin especially, and ate with the family and the Polish neighbour Mister Belinak, who always found a way to get himself invited.

After dinner the children were sent right to bed and my grandmother was thanked for her help, free, for once, to relax in the basement in front of the television set. My grandfather, Mister Addams, and Mister Belinak talked together late into the night, until their stock of hard liquor was totally depleted. For my father, still very young, those evenings were shrouded in a certain mystery. It never entered his mind that they were hidden from his eyes only to spare him the shocking spectacle of seeing his father drunk.

Georges-Émile Archibald didn't drink, except for a porter thick as molasses at Saturday breakfast to go with his eggs and mustard, and, in hiding, in the garage. In the unbridled imagination of my father, these meetings assumed the proportion of Yalta conferences in miniature. The men were clearly making important decisions, either in sharing out the free world or for the better good of those living on Rues Moisan, Castner, and Foucault.

Once, at the hour when the oldsters ought to be retiring to read in bed and the youngsters heading to sleep, my father, without anyone noticing, slipped into the sideboard next to the dining room table, installed himself like a contortionist, and closed himself in. His plan having succeeded, he waited patiently for the evening to reveal its secrets.

In vain.

Made bold by drink, my grandfather, Mister Belinak, and Mister Addams had no more to exchange than dirty jokes, which might have interested my father were he two or three years older. For the time being he understood nothing at all.

The men talked in a kind of drunken Esperanto composed of mispronounced fragments of each other's language, belches, and slaps on the back. My father fell asleep, not knowing that the latch on the door he'd closed was holding him prisoner. It was apparently a good latch, which stood in the way of a logical course of events. Under normal circumstances, my father, his weight bearing forward as he lapsed into sleep, would have forced open the door and fallen to the floor with a thump in front of the guests. Instead, the latch held true, and it was the entire dish-laden cabinet high on its legs that my father dragged with him in his descent. It crashed down on the table, exploding in all directions in splinters of wood and broken glass, almost killing Mister Belinak by fracturing his skull or giving him a heart attack. The men, who had jumped up in unison, stood there dazed for several seconds, before hearing a child weeping beneath the debris.

Usually the story ended there. But on one occasion my father thought good to add this addendum.

We were in the woods, just the two of us, and he said:

"Welsh, my ass. Addams, his real name was Himmler or Goebbels. And Mister Belinak liked him even if he'd killed all his brothers and sisters."

*

The revelation was doubtless apocryphal and a bit forced, but it said what there was to say about our town, that it was a place of refuge where almost everything could be wiped away and forgotten.

Arvida was a town for second chances, undue hopes, and also games.

My grandparents themselves had landed up there in part to hide from their families a shameful secret. My grandfather was a pious man who hadn't sworn twice in his life. He said his rosary at night like an old woman knits. He was a miracle-worker his friends and family phoned from all over, because his prayers stopped bleeding, cured migraines, and helped find lost objects.

The Lord was his shepherd, but my grandfather wasn't made of wood. By subtracting the date of my uncle Clinton's birth from the date of his marriage in the church of Sainte-Thérese, you got something like four months and a bit. My grandmother married pregnant, and my grandparents fled Beauport to expunge the original sin.

As my father said:

"Your grandfather didn't want anyone to know that there was a bit of Rasputin in our saintly Brother André."

*

My grandfather was also a great athlete, and that's what got him invited to Arvida.

It was before colour television and the big networks, Hockey Night and all the tralala, at a time when people had to get their entertainment locally. People in Arvida were mad for sports, outdoor or indoor. They played baseball and softball in the summer. They skated in winter. And all year long you could bowl, see hockey games, or watch wrestling matches at the Community Centre. In the park in front of the big sports complex, you could walk around or sit on a bench in front of a big grandstand where bands and orchestras played.

My grandfather was taken on by Monsieur Latraverse, who was the foreman in Alcan's painting shop, and also a hockey coach. For two years he played hockey all winter and softball all summer, before being hired as an industrial painter in the factory. From then on, my family's destiny was closely bound to this town of leisure and forgetfulness, where anyone could become a saint after having sinned, and where you could achieve local fame as an athlete while waiting for someone to give you a real job.

For a long time, everything went well.

Clinton was born on September 3, 1947.

Hélène on October 20, 1949.

Lise on March 11, 1951.

Douglas, my father, on November 17, 1954.

Georges on May 12, 1956.

Terry, my godfather, on May 25, 1962.

All were good children, and were raised to attend Mass twice a day out of respect for one canonical trinity, and another made up of God, the Montreal Canadiens, and the New York Yankees.

The family flourished in pace with the town, the children grew older, and when they were of an age, the three oldest went off to university.

Signs of exhaustion then began to manifest themselves.

At the age of thirty-nine, my grandmother fell victim to an inexplicable glaucoma and had to be operated on several times so as not to become blind. The operations weakened her considerably, and became more and more delicate, even life-threatening. For weeks, the wives of the bosses and workers delivered food to the terrified husband and children.

During the summer of love, in 1967, my uncle Georges, twelve years old, lost a tooth during the night. Instead of swallowing it, as happens in most such cases, he breathed in the tooth, which rattled around dangerously inside his lungs. He nearly died, and when he recovered, it was to learn that his kidneys were in very bad shape.

It was said that my grandfather never got over that.

My uncle Georges was the quintessence of the Archibald family. He was as bright and studious as the girls, as good a communicator as Clinton, and as brainy, when he applied himself, as Terry, the youngest. He had my father's gift of the gab, and even surpassed him in sports.[4]

---

4   My favourite anecdote, when it comes to my father's sporting fame, is also the earliest. One day, when he was six, my grandfather took him to the neighbourhood skating rink. My father was assigned to the blue team, and he scored eight goals. The other parents were angry and laughing at the same time, and after half an hour it was decided that he would switch teams. After a pause, my father pulled on a red sweater, glided onto the ice, and went on scoring goals as if it was the simplest thing in the world. There were eleven other boys on the ice, four who sent him awkward passes, five who tried to stop him from scoring, one bored goalie, and another who'd developed a gut feeling for what a partridge feels on the first day of hunting season. There were eleven other boys on the ice, on which a beautiful winter sun was shining, and it was as if my father were there all alone, at nightfall, practising his skating and his shots on goal.

My grandfather was bursting with pride. He said to everyone, "That's my son." He blushed and stammered when other fathers congratulated him, he had the same expression as on the spring night he went to knock at my grandmother's door in Beauport, my grandmother who lived with her parents, and he who knocked, bearing his insignificant bouquet of daisies. He had the same expression as when she said, "Yes, that would be nice, let's take a walk." Exactly the same, except that he'd aged.

After a while, the other boys began to have had enough, and to the chagrin of their fathers, they started to behave like children. A little blonde boy began to sob like a sissy because my father had made him trip as he stole the puck from him for the fourth time. Another threw a tantrum because he could never get to touch that damn puck. Yet he was on the same team as my father, and from the stands you couldn't see what he was complaining about. He tried unsuccessfully to shatter his stick by hitting it against the boards, then threw it as far as he could, left the rink, teetering on his skates, and refused to go back on the ice.

When the reds had scored eight goals, it was decided that enough was enough. All the fathers had enjoyed themselves, while all the children left in bad humour. My father included.

He sulked on the way home with his father and big brother, he sulked some more at home sitting at the dining room table, while my grandfather and uncle

It's always a bad omen for a family to see fate bear down on its most illustrious member. The wind was shifting, it's clear, but no one saw it. When he left the hospital, Georges shut himself up in his room and had himself brought down in his armchair to go and pass, hands down, the Ministry exams, making up in a few months all he'd missed over almost two years. He then went back to his room for five months, and to prove the doctors wrong who'd said that he'd never walk again, he came downstairs under his own steam at Christmas and celebrated New Year's on his feet. In many ways, he'd come to embody the Archibald family's resilience.

And so even if the curse was upon them, my grandparents thought that everything would work out. Georges was getting better. Their older children began to have children of their own. Not even twenty-five years old, my father, the most typical Arvidian of the lot, was making money hand over fist with his Bojeans boutiques and his wagers on golf. He owned about half of the hockey and baseball teams in town. Twice a week he went up to Quebec City with Georges for his dialysis. He left him at the Laval University hospital, headed for Montreal to pick up jeans from his warehouses, then returned to the Saguenay, picking up Georges on the way. To entertain us, he brought back from the Parc des Laurentides terrifying

---

recounted his exploits to the rest of the family, describing his sixteen goals one by one, with the verve and precision of the voices on the radio. He sat tight-lipped, with his arms crossed. My grandmother set a steaming plate in front of him, full to the brim, which smelled good, but that he glared at as though it were full of gravel. When my grandmother, who'd pretended not to notice his behaviour for a good quarter of an hour, returned to the table with two more plates, she asked him:

"Dougie, will you please tell me what's wrong with you? You scored sixteen goals this afternoon. How many do you need to make you smile?"

"Yes, I know, mama. I scored sixteen goals. But I didn't win."

In our family ever since, you will find a marked tendency to prefer even catastrophic defeats to tied games.

stories of hitchhikers glimpsed in the wan morning hours, or of strange lights in the sky.

*

It's important to underline: this town whose years of glory I celebrate, I myself only knew it in decline, along with the decline of my own family.

In 1978, the year of my birth, Arvida was administratively fused with Jonquière. On the ground everything looked the same, but its status had changed.

Arvida, a town unto itself, and a model city, no longer existed.

The same year saw both the town's apotheosis and its swan song, a brief burst of brightness at a time when its future was already darkening.

Pierre-Paul Parent, alias Pitou, my father's henchman and my uncle, so to speak, along with the O'Keefe representative Roland Hébert, organized a hockey match that would pitch former Montreal Canadiens against the stars of Arvida's commercial league. Pitou owned the Station, a fashionable bar at the time, which occupied a handsome building on the Rue de Neuville that had once been the Arvida railway station, and today is a funeral home.

In the opposing ranks were Jean-Guy Talbot, Henri Richard, Claude Provost, Gilles Marotte, Ken Mosdell, and many others. In the nets, I believe, was the former Rangers goalie Gilles Villemure. The coach and manager of the team, who during the exhibition games served as referee, was Maurice Richard, the Rocket. Pitou appointed himself scorekeeper and house announcer.

The Arvida players were no pushovers. All had played at least to the Junior level, including my father, who wasn't playing at that point because he'd hurt his knee and my mother was pregnant, but the family legend was that he'd had his nose broken by Guy Lafleur at the Remparts camp a few years earlier.

Among them, Yvon Bouchard had played in Europe, and Mauril Morisette and Réjean Maltais in the American League, while Germain Gagnon had made the Islanders camp in New York. All represented the fragile memory of a time when the balance of power wasn't yet predetermined, when the far corners of the countryside produced humble athletes as good, if not better, than those in the urban centres.

An important page in regional history was written, in fact, when in February 1910, the Canadiens hockey team came to contest an exhibition game against the Chicoutimi Hockey Club. The Canadiens, led by the marksmen Didier Pitre and Newsy Lalonde, were unable to score a single goal against the legendary Georges Vezina. They lost 11-0, and left, their tails between their legs, but with an important consolation prize: Vezina himself, who tended their nets for sixteen seasons, only to die, just like that, from a coughing fit, before having blown out even forty birthday candles.

Of course, no one was going to abscond with a major league club after the match at the Community Centre. The dreams of glory had had their day, and the former Canadiens, in any case, hadn't even arrived by bus. They'd come down in a cavalcade, four by four in big Buicks, Molsons tucked between their legs. That was no reason to knuckle under, certainly. And it was no accident that the Arvidian who led the assault was himself a goalie, and doubtless the player who'd come closest to a career in the National Hockey League. Claude Hardy had played in the AHL for the Springfield Kings and the Rochester Americans, had played several games in the NHL, but had decided to swap his dreams of glory for the love of a woman and a job as fireman that his father and a priest had found for him.

He still loved his wife and the job, but he missed the glory. From the start of the match, before three thousand people at the Community Centre, Hardy adopted a super-aggressive style verging on mental imbalance, akin to that of Gerry Cheevers, or the approach popularized later by Ron Hextall. He shot out of his goal like a wild man, skated far from the neutral zone to renew the attack, and aimed great hatchet blows with his stick at anyone coming too close to his net.

Above all he played goal. The shots that the former Canadiens in vacation mode lobbed in his direction ended up in his mitt, under his pads, diverted into the stands, everywhere but in the net.

At the end of the first period, the score was 3-0 for Arvida. Hardy seemed to have lit a fire under his teammates, one that had long been dormant. The crowd, packed shoulder to shoulder, was jubilant, and the Canadiens seemed not to know what had hit them. They'd come to have fun and be served a free meal. Most were playing bare-headed with their locks smoothed back to charm the local beauties, and perhaps to entice one of them into their room at the Richelieu Motel. Now their hair was a mess and they were bleeding from the nose.

They didn't like that, nor did the Rocket and nor did Pitou, who hadn't struggled to entice these sports legends to Arvida just to have them beat up on. He tore a strip off the players in the locker room during the first break, reminding them that they wanted to fill the arena and his bar afterwards, that they wanted a great party and money to finance the league, not a bloody Saint Valentine's massacre.

He ended by saying:

"Come on. These guys are our heroes."

And that's when Hardy, sitting bent over, staring at a point on the ground between his pads, super concentrated, raised his eyes to Pitou and replied:

"Heroes my ass."[5]

No one added a word, and Pitou left the room, cursing.

The second period was more difficult for the Arvida stars, who bled from the nose in their turn. The Habs had woken up, and the Rocket, as referee, showed himself to be very parsimonious with his whistle when his former teammates pounded the locals into the boards. Pitou himself, as scorekeeper, played free and easy with the time, favouring the legends, terminating their penalties with undue alacrity, and dragging out those imposed on his obstinate fellow Arvidians.

And yet the Arvidians held their ground. Hardy especially. He gave up three goals, but stopped an improbable number of hard shots, while driving the crowd wild. He raised his arms in the air and saluted them. When the action shifted to the other end, he pulled a comb out of his mitt and adjusted the part on the side of his head, like a little punk. The spectators howled with laughter. Towards the fifteenth minute of the second period, Henri Richard got a breakaway while Hardy was doing his little stunt. Hardy let Richard come at him without putting his helmet back on, his head held high like that of an ancient warrior. Richard waited until he was just the right distance away, and unleashed a vicious slap shot that Hardy grabbed a nanosecond later, sweeping his arm around in a wide arc. The

---

5   Only that's not what he said in French. He said "*Héros de ma queue,*" which means "Heroes my... prick? cock?" Whatever. Had he said "Heroes my ass," it would have come out "*Héros de mon cul.*" It was common in Arvida, in the somewhat coarse milieu of my father, in any case, to replace the traditional "*de mon cul*" by "*de ma queue.*" Implicit in the expression is the awareness that the appendage in question is both the only thing a man possesses of which he is the sole owner, and the wellspring of all his misfortunes. An interesting variant consists in replacing the possessive "my" (*ma*) with a "your" (*ta*), while tacking an ending onto someone else's sentence, usually to cut short any hint of boastfulness.

"Things going well at work, Jean Guy?"

"Oh yes, very well. They've just named me manager."

"*De ta queue.*"

puck slammed into his mitt with a hollow plop, like a burst of buckshot into a pillow.

That's when Hardy committed the most Saguenayan act I've ever seen in my life. Courageous, grand, arrogant, and in the end utterly stupid. Before the referee could even blow his whistle, Hardy dropped the puck and slid it towards Richard, as if to say, "Here, have another go." It took Henri Richard two or three seconds to grasp the significance of the gesture, after which he charged Hardy, letting his gloves fall to the ice. The brawl became general, and while the crowd noisily voiced its elation, Maurice Richard, the rocket, skated to the scorer's box near the penalty bench, and said to Pitou:

"Hey. We're not here to be laughed at."

The Habs added another goal after the fight, and the teams went back to their locker rooms with the score 5-4 for the locals. Pitou apologized to Maurice, and, confident, went to join the players. He had a plan.

The substitute goalie for the Arvida stars was Rémy Bouchard, caretaker for the high school, and tavern keeper. For him it was an honorary position, because he'd done a lot for the league and the team. He was a good-humoured fellow, liked by all. It was said that he could drink a twelve-pack in less than forty-five minutes, and that he kept his goalie equipment all year long in the back of his pickup, so that it smelled of mould and cat piss. In his entire life, however, he'd never stopped anything, neither a puck nor a beach ball.

Pitou convinced the players that during the third period Rémy should guard the goal vis à vis the idols of his youth. The idea wasn't hard to sell, because everyone liked Rémy, and they'd had enough of Claude Hardy's immoderate behaviour.

And so the third period began with Rémy Bouchard in goal, and no one on the bench in the goalie's spot. Still in the locker room, Hardy had repaired to the showers.

The Habs were out for blood and everyone expected that the exploit of the commercial league's stars was nearing its end. As soon as the puck dropped, the Canadiens took control. Talbot coaxed Bouchard like a rookie towards his right, and flipped a beautiful quick pass to Henri Richard on the left. He rifled a shot towards the empty slot that was at least as powerful as the one he'd launched at Hardy in the second period.

Then something strange happened.

With a swan's grace, Rémy Bouchard made a lateral move of improbable fluidity towards his left, stretched out his arm as far as it would reach, and intercepted the puck with the tip of his mitt. In the stands, the silence was total. Bouchard brought his right leg behind his left, and with great dignity pulled himself erect facing the crowd in a pose that seemed more appropriate to a fencer than a goalie. The ovation burst out, and Pitou Parent beside the penalty bench dropped his head onto the table, murmuring, "Oh my god."

Maurice Richard came up to him one more time to shout in his ear:

"So you've brought us here just to screw us around."

And Pitou, who'd dreamed of meeting the man ever since he was a little boy, heard himself answer, in sadness, and almost despite himself:

"You know what, Rocket? Go fuck yourself."

I don't know how, but whatever was on fire in Hardy became an inferno in Rémy. He who had been at best a mediocre goalie, found himself stopping pucks with his mask, with his behind, with his calves, with his back, and even with his elbows. He blocked shots while trying to dodge them, blocked them while falling on the ground, blocked them while looking to the heavens to pray that he be spared from them. Yvon Bouchard turned to his brother Laurent, and said:

"Jesus. We're going to win."

And indeed they won. The Canadiens made twenty-three shots on Rémy in the third period, and only two got through. His inspired teammates scored three more.

Final score: 8 to 6.

Pitou, even if he was angry with the Rocket, did everything he could to help his guests, unduly drawing out the third period, which, according to modest estimates, lasted fifty-five minutes. In the end, in any case, good humour prevailed. With his burlesque performance, which amused even his adversaries, who in friendly fashion came to tap him on his pads after each of his improbable stops, Rémy had done a lot to pacify the match.

Pitou, for his part, had done much to transform it into a circus. It was, after all, the end of the seventies, and Pitou, like everyone, had a slight drug problem. House announcer and self-appointed scorekeeper, he told himself that the little cubicle set aside for those functions would make a perfect hiding place, enabling him to drink his beer in peace and to do a line from time to time. In fact, in an arena where hundreds of spectators could look right down on him, this was without doubt the worst hiding place imaginable. But Pitou wasn't going to be discouraged by such a small detail. He sniffed away in full view of everybody, made numerous errors on the board, which he was slow in correcting, and accounted for the exodus of several outraged parents. From the middle of the second period on he was practically inaudible, and garbled the names of scorers before assigning assists to players who were absent, if not deceased. Confused, senior citizens in the stands started murmuring in their neighbours' ears:

"Eh, what? Elmer Lach's here?"

On the ice, however, the Canadiens and Arvidians were now enjoying themselves, fellow feeling having come to the fore with Claude Hardy's departure.

They celebrated until late, legends and stars together. Rémy Bouchard was awarded the game's first star. As is often the case with true heroes, Hardy fêted his exploit all alone at home, banished from the party thanks to his Homeric, moronic gesture. The local paper the next day paid tribute to the evening overall, while censuring the lapses in sportsmanship early in the match, and the shameful conduct of the organizer.

A low blow Pitou never forgave the journalist, not to the day of his death on December 4, 2010.

*

The next year, my grandfather went to consult his doctor for a pain in his thumb, and learned that he had contracted amyotrophic lateral sclerosis, a degenerative disease that would carry him off sooner or later. He wept a lot, and spent much of his time over the following years sitting in an armchair kneading his rosary. It's said that a little boy stayed near him all the time, and helped him to find the right position on a cushion where he might rest his stiffened ankles. I have no memory of this, but the little boy was me.

He died in 1981, not having forgotten to remind all and sundry that his condition, in the United States, had another name: Lou Gehrig's disease. What killed my grandfather had also killed the New York Yankees' iron man.

My grandmother was the sole inheritor of the house and her ailing son. She'd never drunk a drop in her life, but in secret she'd taken to downing great glassfuls of whatever was at hand, taken from the bar at any time of day. I know that, because she often babysat my brother and myself, and her eyes were no longer sharp enough to see me hidden beyond her peripheral vision. She liked watching over us a lot, my grandmother. She cooked as if trying to fatten us up, but as we were running around outside all the time, nothing stuck to our bones. At noon hour on school days, we went to her house to eat a quick sandwich, and to play cards.

She called my brother, whose eyes are not green, the little man with apple-green eyes. She called me her angel with horns.

In the winter of 2001, my father ran for councillor in Arvida in the municipal elections. He'd set up his campaign office in the abandoned locale of the Orlac Jewellers on Davis Square, right beside the Arvida Brasserie. Pitou Parent was the informal strategist and press attaché. The last weekend before the vote, my Uncle Clinton picked me up on my way down from Ottawa. Then, passing through Quebec City, we picked up my friend Phil Leblanc. Clinton's plan was to go door to door with my father, canvassing the old Arvida families. For Phil, me, and Marc Laganiére, who was waiting for us on site, it was a matter of phoning people on the list whom we were likely to know, from eighteen to thirty years old.

Things didn't go very well, and this is not a story I enjoy telling. It was a dismal end-of-winter, the lawns were yellowed, and everything and everyone was drenched in a scuzzy drizzle. My father had lost about thirty pounds, and was as nervous as a cat. He took me into a corner to hand me a little jar of medicine, nitro pills that our seventy-year-old friend Ti-Bi had given him, totally illegally. My father told me that I had to quickly slip a pill under his tongue should he have a blackout, something that had happened once or twice during the campaign.

A single photo remains from that lost weekend, showing us sitting around a table, Clinton, my father, Marc, Phil, and myself. Pale from the winter and ashen from fatigue, bags under our eyes and our hair in a mess, we look like vampires. I mean real vampires, out of an old Slavic legend from before there was printing.

Strigoi sitting around a forty-ounce bottle of Chivas Regal.

On election Sunday, in the evening, I took my place as scrutineer at the Sainte-Thérèse neighbourhood polling centre in the Saguenay Valley School's tiny gymnasium, just a few steps from my grandmother's old house. The results were not good. I left before the last ballots were counted. I knew perfectly well that if the situation was so bad there, at the heart of our territory, it would be disastrous elsewhere. And it was. My father had to shoulder two jobs for a year to pay back the costs of his campaign.

I brought my bad news to the headquarters with little hurried steps, under the rain. I crossed Boulevard des Saguenéens and the lawn of the Notre-Dame-du-Sourire primary school, trudged through its gravelly playground and up the old coulee path, before coming out beside the Palace.

In that landscape of my childhood, I told myself that I would never again confuse the mythic Arvida, over which my family had reigned in my dreams since 1947, with the municipality of the same name, in the Saguenay.

Here, I mean there, we were kings of nothing, princes of our sorry backsides.

In many respects, the exile had begun long before.

In 1993 my grandmother left the Saguenay and returned to Beauport, from which her sisters had never strayed very far, and where her son Georges and his wife Maud were then installed.

The last time I saw her was in 2002. She was in a hospital room in Quebec City, and was not wearing her glasses. As in an old engraving, she was staring with bulging eyes at the emptiness over her bed, as though an incubus were hovering there with its black wings spread wide. The hospital was one of those beautiful old Quebec buildings that take you back in time despite yourself, with ghostly good sisters coming at you around a bend in the corridor, and visitors wondering whatever happened to their hats and their gaiters.

It was winter, and I have no memory of the view from the window. Perhaps the curtains were drawn, it seems to me that it was very dark. We'd spent the afternoon there with my aunts

Lise and Hélène. Both of them doctors, they were engaged in an ongoing struggle with their male colleagues to have the doses increased. Those men no longer went to Mass or crossed themselves when a priest passed by, but curiously, they still believed that there was some grace to be found in suffering.

At one point, a lovely nurse about forty years old, energetic and sexy, came into the room to adjust my grandmother in her bed and to see if everything was going well. She tried to make conversation with her by asking her who were the people with her. My grandmother pointed to my aunts, saying with pride that they were her two daughters, both doctors.

The nurse added:

"And those two handsome boys, who are they, Madame Archibald?"

My grandmother stared at us for a long time, as if she'd never seen us in her life, and she said, in a panic:

"I don't know, my grand nephews I think. Or little cousins."

My Aunt Lise laughed nervously.

"No, mama. They're David and Sam, Dougie's sons."

My grandmother put her hand to her brow and said she was tired. She then shifted her gaze to the unseen exterminator perched over her bed. She breathed a long sigh.

My Aunt Hélène, a lung specialist who nevertheless shared our nicotine addiction, took us aside and said:

"Let's go smoke a cigarette, boys, we'll let your grandmother sleep."

Outside, Hélène and Lise explained that our grandmother would have forgotten them as well, had they not been at her bedside for two weeks. She only remembered the names of her children because they had been dictated to her. She remembered the Beauport of her youth, of her own beauty, and of her fiancé Georges-Émile. She talked about her sisters Marielle, Nicole, Georgette, and Monique, and of her sisters-in-law, Nyna, Mabel, Maude, and Gemma, who had become her good friends. She remembered her childhood and adolescence and her whole life up to her marriage, but she'd forgotten Arvida.

At that point, I should have understood that in fact there was nothing more Arvidian than to forget Arvida itself. I should have understood that I was myself free to leave it forever, because in any case I was incapable of forgetting anything at all. But I was too young. And my brother and I were devastated.

Lise told us that our grandmother remembered the time when her life was her own, before in Arvida it became that of others. In Arvida her life had been that of her children, then of the priests who came to eat with the family on Sunday, then of the little hockey players, atom, peewee, and bantam, then of her sick son and her sick husband, then of David and me when our parents had divorced.

We shouldn't be upset that she'd forgotten us, she said. She no longer remembered anything of her life with us in Arvida because that life, she'd already given us.

I looked at my brother. The only intelligent thing I found to say, which was not really intelligent when I think of it, came right out of the language of sports, those rough recreations in which the Arvidians of the entire world batter their bodies, while in their heads make short work of everything they can't forget.

I said, in English:

"Nice try, but no cigar."

She died the next day, my grandmother, mother of my father.

Her body lay in repose during all of the month of January. After, when the ground had thawed in the Saguenay, they brought her back to Arvida to bury her beside my grandfather.

The Last-Born

GOD KNOWS how he could get it into his head that two thousand dollars would be enough for him to kill somebody. What does it mean, after all, a sum like that? He could easily have worked it out, Raisin, he always spent in multiples of twenty. Two thousand dollars was never more than two hundred cases of beer / a hundred nights at the movies if you counted the popcorn, the Pepsi and the bus / thirty or so half-hours in the little room with the girls from the topless bar who never charged him like the others when they did consent to take his money. They arrived from everywhere those girls, on the three a.m. bus that left them off in front of the gas station, mostly on Wednesdays. From time to time Raisin stayed up late and hung around to watch the new ones disembark. There were three or four per week. Lots of Blacks for the last two years. The clients weren't too happy about that, people didn't go much for Blacks around here. But he liked them a lot. The girls had beautiful fat asses, little breasts with big black nipples, they sprayed themselves with a revolting scent, part pine oil, part bubble gum, but Raisin dreamed that it smelled of the far away, the not here. For him this was the aroma of Africa and Haiti, and the smell was good. A lot better in any case than the odour of the pulp and paper mill that lingered in the air in the heat of summer, and that the faintest breeze wafted abroad, pristine and potent, for kilometres round about. The locals were used to it, but not him, the smell lodged in his nostrils, stuck to his palate, a ghastly stench of rotten eggs.

He could have tallied it any old way, but try to figure how such minds work.

There were about a dozen of them, the last-born, all burdened with a nickname they hated, born into old-style families to aging ladies who ought to have stopped having children long before, but whose husbands and priests never gave them any peace as long as there was one egg left in their innards. Their brothers and sisters had left town to become doctors and lawyers or else had stuck around and found work in the factory, like their fathers. These were all getting close to retirement. As for the last-born, they never strayed very far. A few had just reached their forties, and lived at home with their parents until the parents died. After, their brothers and sisters pocketed the money from the house sale, and the last-born went to live on their disability pensions or their welfare cheques in low-rent lodgings, apartment blocks or semi-basements, at the four corners of the town.

They made it through the month doing odd jobs. From time to time, in the summer, on the first of the month, at the neighbourhood fairs or when some of them had made more money than expected on a little rebuilding contract, they got drunk. They were found in the morning, asleep in the town's parks or on strangers' lawns, fallen in action on the return trip by foot or bicycle. Raisin was one of the better coordinated: most often they found him on the same lawn, that of the Laberges, in the same position (an improbable intertwining of his limbs with the wheels and frame of his old ten-speed), barely the worse for wear or miraculously untouched. The Laberges were affable and gentle folks, once friends to his parents. They never woke him. It was July's burning sun or the chill of late August mornings that brought him back to life and sent him wobbling homeward.

None of the last-born were truly cretins or morons, even if that's what giggling children sometimes accused them of on their way out of school. None of them were Nobel prize-winners in chemistry either. In those parts, people sometimes said that someone was "not nasty enough to start a fire, but also not bright enough to put it out." That was not a bad depiction of the last-born. There was no raving madman in their ranks, no one severely handicapped mentally, but they were all lacking in some small thing.

Bozzo, up to Grade 10, had been good at arithmetic and dictation, but he couldn't finish a sentence if his life depended on it. He knew just what he wanted to say, took a deep breath, started to speak, but after a few words had to stop short. Syntax shrivelled up in his mouth and ideas unthreaded in his mind as soon as he tried to relay them from his neurons to his vocal chords. He could only express himself in puny little sentence fragments, and most of the time opted to laugh or grunt. Or swear. Swearing was practical, with the right inflection it could say all sorts of things, and in just one word. He would put several end to end without losing track. Jesus Christ goddamn piss-all fuckshit son of a bitch.

Minou had the clearest skin, the bluest eyes, and the most sublime face a man could have, but even when his mother was absent he was not the sharpest member of the household, which also included three cats, a poodle, and a king parrot. Among the last-born he was the youngest, and perhaps the only one who would not be left to his own devices when his mother died. Minou was a total ninny. What was odd was that on festive occasions, when his mother dressed him up in a good suit, he looked like a model. He was so comely that from time to time young women refused to admit to themselves that he hadn't changed, even when they saw all the signs. Once, at a Dubé boy's baptism, a lady led him behind a shed, took hold of his hand, and slid it under her skirt and between her legs, until

Minou's fingers made contact with her unclad sex. Minou took off wailing like one possessed, and he was found two days later rolled into a ball under a fir tree on the golf course, almost ten kilometres away.

Caboche had a head too big for his body and always had to lean it against something when he was seated, otherwise it could drop down and pop his vertebrae. The year before, while he was caddying for the Knights of Columbus classic golf tournament, an exceptionally long drive by the notary Lalonde had bounced off the top of his skull. That hadn't helped at all.

Jambon was a chatterbox and an epileptic.

Popeye talked a lot as well, except that what he said was always inaudible, even more so when he drank and appeared to be expressing himself in a foreign language.

Among the last-born, Raisin was the most cunning, and he was strong as a horse. That gave him a certain prestige, because he was the one who worked the most. The only problem was his fingers. They were like thick carrot stubs, and just as useless. You couldn't do much with fingers like that, not typing at a machine or playing the piano, not even digging in your nose. Once he'd got hold of an object, he could lift it and manipulate it almost normally until it dropped from his hands. He was called on for house moving, for mowing lawns, or outside renovation jobs. He was reputed to be good for "heavy work."

For ten years he'd taken care of his sick mother as well as his clumsy fingers would allow. During all that time people had sympathy for him, then pity. When his mother died and his brothers and sisters decided to sell the house, Monsieur Blackburn had offered him, for a modest sum, the small apartment he'd fixed up in his basement. Raisin had accepted. The Blackburns let him entertain up to three guests on the front balcony, and when they left on vacation they let him swim in the pool. Raisin made modest use of these privileges. He rarely authorized the last-born to join him and preferred hanging out with them on the baseball field. He was more likely to invite his most troubled clients, those who were always looking for somewhere they could drink out of range of their wives. He also invited Martial, who was not married, often hung around the brasserie, and liked talking to Raisin, who enjoyed listening to him.

In the neighbourhood, you didn't talk about "bikers," about "gangsters," or about "organized crime," but about the "*gaffe*." Martial wasn't a real member of the gaffe, but he'd hovered about it for a long time. He did little jobs for the guys in the gaffe, deliveries, driving, that kind of thing. From time to time they let him deal in small quantities of drugs, and in his free time he got involved in all sorts of schemes, and broke into houses to steal television sets or jewellery. He'd also done a bit of prison. He was small, scrawny, and nervous. He had blonde hair, long and greasy, little faded tattoos on each forearm, and joints that stuck out like broken bottles.

That's probably how it all came about, in fact. Martial had spent his life imagining he was tough enough to order up a murder, and Raisin, who had tolerated ten years of pitying looks from all and sundry while he was taking care of his mother, would swill the aftertaste of pity out of his mouth by imagining that he was capable of killing someone. The two were made for each other.

In any case, one evening, while they were talking quietly on the steps of the Blackburns, Martial let slip:

"That asshole Sanguinet, I wish he were dead."

Raisin replied:

"I could take care of that."

There was silence. Martial began to perspire. He didn't quite know what to say. His only thought was to ask:

"Would you do it for two thousand?"

And Raisin replied:

"Yes. Five hundred now and the rest after."

They'd just taken a big step. A kind of moronic one, obviously, but a step all the same. Two normal people would have changed their minds, would have found a way to unsay what had been said while still saving face, but not them. Their whole relationship was a sham. Each one told himself, through the mediation of the other, that he was more dangerous than people thought, that he wasn't just a petty crook and a simple soul. They could have gone on pretending to be tough. To have made believe that the conversation had never taken place, and to have kept on telling themselves that they were really the sort to talk that way. They could have, but, in truth, that would have made huge demands on their respective capacities for abstraction.

They parted with a handshake, and each went his way, stepping briskly, to the rhythm of two hearts beating wildly in their rib cages.

Raisin had pondered the question for a long time. His father had owned a small .22 calibre long gun for years, never registered. It was in a closet in the basement, stored in its case along with an old box of bullets. When his mother died, Raisin was able to hide the rifle and save it from being sold off. No one in the family, or outside it, knew about its existence. He could easily kill someone with it and go somewhere to bury it. What was crucial, and this he'd learned from cop films, was never to be caught with the gun.

And so Sanguinet was going to die, because he'd refused to let Martial, after the deadline, change his bet on a football match, he who insisted in betting on sports even if he knew nothing about them, and kept on asking Sanguinet to alter his bets even though he knew the bookmaker couldn't do so.

Sanguinet was a professional bookmaker and gambler. He held the bets on all the international sporting matches, and had feelers out everywhere that enabled him to lay money on local games. He also sold contraband cigarettes. He was the kind of harmless criminal that respectable men like to associate with, so as to mix with the underworld at little cost. The police never made trouble for him, never made him open the trunk of his Buick; several of them placed bets with him, and some smoked his cigarettes.

He was virtually a last-born. He was an only child at a time when families were still large, born of the curious union of a factory worker who arrived out of nowhere one filthy January night, and a woman whom he presented as his wife, but who strangely resembled him, and who for a long time was rumoured to be his sister. His father and mother were tall and bony, he was fleshy and short in stature. He'd lived with his parents until their death, and had never really worked.

He spent his days going back and forth between his clients' houses and an assortment of bars. At night he sat on his porch behind the house, which gave on the woods that separated the golf course from the water purification plant. When a client had to find him he met him there, or knocked on the windows of the patio door if Sanguinet was watching television inside.

For a few days Raisin made a study of how he spent his time. One night, at an ungodly hour when good people were sleeping, Raisin went out with his rifle in hand and wound his way through alleyways and yards, trying not to rouse the dogs. He himself knocked on the glass. When Sanguinet opened the door, he managed, despite his nerves and clumsy hands, to shoot off the gun and fire a round into the gambler's midriff.

Beyond that, Raisin had no plan. He'd not foreseen the noise of the discharge that jolted everyone awake nearby, nor the dumbfounded look that Sanguinet gave him after falling on his behind through the vertical blinds, to land on the dining room floor. Raisin had assumed he'd be capable of killing Sanguinet because he didn't much like people, though he liked animals and would never have caused any harm to a cat or a pup. Unfortunately for him, that's exactly what Sanguinet looked like with his blood-stained hands clutching his perforated belly, and his eyes wide open with fear.

Raisin tossed the gun into the flower bed, took Sanguinet in his arms as if he weighed nothing at all, and carried him, running, to the hospital, twenty minutes away, without pausing for a moment.

The small calibre bullet hadn't caused much damage. They extracted it from Sanguinet's abdomen and let him rest until the next day. Raisin stayed in the waiting room all during the operation, then spent part of the night at the wounded man's bedside. No one could get him to say anything, nor make him understand that it was time to leave, nor even make him budge. No one, until the police arrived. They'd been alerted by the doctor on duty, who had to report any bullet wounds. Unable to get anything out of him, they handcuffed Raisin and put him in preventive detention, pending some clarification of what had occurred.

Constable Leduc couldn't talk to Sanguinet until the next afternoon. Sanguinet immediately asked him where Raisin was.

"We've placed him under observation. He was in a state of shock. Is he the one who shot you?"

"Yes, but it was an accident. Go to my house, he must have left the gun there. It belonged to my father. I wasn't sure whether I should register it or throw it away, so I asked Raisin to come and help me see if it was still working. That's how it happened. We were sure it wouldn't fire. Raisin must have forgotten to remove the bullet that was in the chamber, and when we went to close it up, it went off.

"Why did you ask Raisin to help you?

"He's my friend."

"You're Raisin Tremblay's friend? That's news to me."

"Aw, you know what I mean. He helps me with my rock garden in front, I give him some painting contracts, things like that. Sometimes he comes over for a beer. He knows about guns."

"Raisin Tremblay knows nothing about anything. And are you going to tell me why you'd ask a semi-retard to help you try out your rifles at two in the morning?"

"I know, I know. It wasn't a good idea."

The two men stared at each other.

"Do you have any more questions?"

Leduc cleared his throat.

"Are you sure you don't have any other answers to give me?"

Sanguinet kept to his story, and later that day, after having been released, he went to pick up Raisin at the police station. They didn't exchange a word during the trip. Sanguinet left him off in front of the Blackburns and said goodbye, but Raisin got out of the car and went in without saying a word.

That night, Raisin took part of Martial's five hundred dollars and went to buy a lot of beer at the corner store. He walked as far as the baseball field, where for the time being there was no last-born in sight, sat on the players' bench, and downed, one by one, the twenty-four bottles in the case. Zigzagging home, he looked like a domestic bull to which one had administered a powerful sedative. At the steps to the Blackburns, his cat, which had again run off, was rolled into a ball in front of the door. Raisin grabbed the cat by the skin of its neck, kicked open the door, and heaved it inside. In the air, the terrorized animal, which was not a cat but a skunk, emptied its sphincters full force, showering Raisin and the walls with a foul liquid, part ammonia and part excrement.

Raisin felt sick, he wept from the pain and the sadness, and didn't know what to do. He reeled, reeking, the three blocks to

Sanguinet's house, and knocked at the door. Sanguinet opened it, and without giving him a chance to dodge his embrace and the odour that came along with it, Raisin sobbed in his arms for a good half hour.

They spent part of the night cleaning Sanguinet's house, slept for a few hours, with Raisin on the couch and Sanguinet in the bedroom, and on waking they went together to disinfect the Blackburns' so they wouldn't have to face the nauseating smell when they returned from their vacation.

From that point on, Sanguinet began to take Raisin with him on his rounds. The word was that Sanguinet had decided that Raisin's big fists could be good for something, and that he'd made him his collector. In fact, Sanguinet never asked Raisin to beat up anyone, never mind to kill somebody. And he never even asked him why he'd come knocking at his door that night with a rifle in his hands.

The next year, during the summer, without thinking, Martial, who'd tried hard to forget the whole story and given up for good on getting his five hundred dollars back, let his feet guide him to the front of the Blackburn house. Sanguinet and Raisin were there on the stoop, beers in hand, watching the sun go down behind the backstop. Raisin waved to him.

"Hey, Martial."

Martial froze and broke out in a sweat. He waved back.

"How ya doing, boys?"

Sanguinet offered:

"Come have a beer with us, Martial."

Martial still hesitated, then, not knowing what else to do, he sat down beside them.

The night was soft and calm, and you could hear the stomachs of Raisin and Martial as they gurgled in the evening air. At first, all three sucked on their beers in silence, then the conversation found its rhythm. They talked about the weather, the sports scores, and the enticing neckline of a barmaid at the brasserie. Subjects that seemed to have been invented, that night, just for them, just so people like them might have something to talk about.

House Bound

HARDLY ANYONE believes me, but when I bought the house in 1993 it had settled so far down that I had to take eighteen inches off the height of each wall before shoring up the foundations. I revved up my chainsaw right in the middle of the living room and carved away like a madman, just watching so as not to slice through any load-bearing beams. It was no big deal because in the beginning it was all mine to fix up. A lot of people said "That couldn't be," and I don't blame them because there are lots of stories that are hard to fathom when it comes to that house.

When I saw it for the first time it was on behalf of a client. Armand Sénécal. He was going to buy it, and he asked me to inspect it first. I came along Rue Forster, turned up the driveway with its five hundred-year-old trees on each side, and parked in the turnaround at the end, right in front of an imposing residence that seemed really small under the trees. I let out a whistle, sitting alone in the car. I loved that house at first sight, and then a bit more with each defect I found there that would put Armand off. The roof was a disaster, and I would have bet anything that what was just under it was rotten too. The second and third floor walls showed clear signs of water infiltration. The basement was a humid cave, and you could tell just by the smell that the French drain was clogged. The tennis court in the back was nice, but it had been left untended for at least ten years. And then there was the icing on the cake. All across the property there were things the agent tried to pass off as sculptures, but that looked like junk picked up in a scrapyard: steel rods wrapped in barbed wire in the middle of a flower bed; big sheets of iron and copper soldered to look like African masks and fastened to stakes here and there on the front lawn; beside the tennis court there was an old yellow bus planted upright in the ground, with five big tractor wheels around it. A yellow bus sticking straight up in the air, I swear on my daughter's head.

Apparently the house belonged to the Villeneuve family, town notables who'd owned a number of businesses in the region, beginning with a rock quarry lower down on the hill, towards the Saguenay. Armand said there was an old path starting behind the house, which brought you there on foot. The house was the family's summer home from about the 1910s to the 1960s. The last residents were Viateur Villeneuve, his wife Claire, and their four children. Old man Villeneuve was a pretty well-known local artist. He'd taught at the trade school, where they did woodwork and cabinetmaking. The children were gone, the old man was dead, and now Madame Villeneuve wanted to sell the house, which was too big for her.

I asked Armand:

"How much does she want for it, Madame Villeneuve?"

"Two hundred and fifty thousand."

"Well, if you pay two hundred and fifty thousand for that, you can be sure of two things. First, you're going to regret it, and second, I'm going to go all over town telling everyone 'Armand Sénécal has a heart of gold.'"

Saying that about anyone around here is not exactly a compliment. Armand swore under his breath, then said:

"How much would you give, at the most?"

"A hundred and eighty five, maybe a hundred and ninety thousand. That's if I had two hundred thousand more to sink into the renovations, and ten years of my life to spare."

He thanked me, and we each went our way. Two days later, Madame Villeneuve, in person, called me at my office. She sang me a chorus of insults. She even tacked on some *"crisses"* and *"tabarnacs"* that coming from her had the ring of responses committed to memory for Mass. When she'd finished her bit of theatre, I put in, "Madame Villeneuve, I'm going to tell you something. Your house, I want it. I'm going to give you a hundred thousand dollars for it, with a disclaimer clause in the act of sale. That way you'll be sure that I'll never go after you for a hidden defect. Talk to some people with their heads on straight, if you know any. They'll tell you that you'll never get more than that."

She hung up in my face. The next week I passed in front of the house, I turned around in the driveway, and I stopped the car. I found the house beautiful, with its roof broken up by attic windows, the grey asphalt shingles peeling away on top, the two dormers projecting from the front façade, the large cedar shutters, and the hoary whitewashed walls. I couldn't help myself.

I saw Madame Villeneuve peering out the window, through the curtains. I took off immediately. As if I felt guilty. I breathed a long sigh and for once decided to listen to the voice that always talks into my ear, telling me what to do, and that now was saying, "Forget it."

A year later, I was living elsewhere. I'd just finished moving with my wife and little girl into a house that I wasn't crazy about, but that would do us for a while. The telephone rang. It was the good woman Villeneuve.

"Do you remember me?"

"Yes, Madame. What can I do for you?"

"I'd like to know if your offer still holds."

The truth was, that it didn't. I'd just transferred everything into the new house, and moved my office. But business was good, and I knew that it wouldn't take long for me to refill my coffers. I also knew that if Madame Villeneuve were calling me now, it was because she'd spent a good year trying to sell her house.

I said:

"Yes, Madame, it still holds. Except that I can't give you the money for at least three months. I'll need time to sell my house here."

"I understand. That seems reasonable."

"But there's one more thing: I'm not going to move my wife and daughter into your shithouse without doing a minimum of renovation."

She coughed.

"What are you saying?"

"I'd like you out within two weeks."

"You want to pay me in six months and turf me out today. Is that it?"

"Right."

"Can I think about it?"

"Take your time, Madame."

That time I was the one who hung up. It was her son who called me two weeks later. He'd had the papers drawn up, and he was anxious for me to sign. He was in the Saguenay for just one week, enough time to move his mother into a retirement home and liquidate her possessions. At the notary's, he offered to leave me the furniture or the objects already in place. I replied that they could keep their old rubbish, and that they were lucky I wasn't charging them to remove the old man's rusty totems from my property. I then asked him, just to make conversation, if his mother had had him close the deal because she was sick, and he replied:

"It's not that, no. She says you're the coarsest person she's ever met in her life."

That same afternoon, I went to see the empty house. It was there and it was mine. My humble abode. I'd always dreamed of a house like that, and now I had it. It would take me five, ten, twenty years to fix it up the way I wanted, but that didn't matter because I'd dreamed for forty years of putting my family into a house like that.

No one believes me, but I managed not to say anything to my wife and daughter for quite a while. I sold the other house through contacts, scheduling visits for when my wife and daughter were out. For five months I did the work in secret, contracting out a few of the jobs. After a while my wife began to think I had a new mistress. I had the tennis court in the back taken out and a swimming pool dug, I had the foundations set right, and I plastered over the strips I'd taken out with the chainsaw. I restored the outside walls and had them painted yellow, a beautiful bright yellow, a bit mustardy, to contrast with the green shingles I'd installed on the roof. I dismantled old man Villeneuve's sculptures and sold off the pieces as scrap. A lot of people called me a barbarian for doing that, but I have to say that I offered them for free to all the museums in the region as long as they'd come to cart them away, and not one said yes. I painted inside as well. My friends came to help me out from time to time, and at the end I think the whole town knew I'd bought the house except for my wife and my little girl.

One Sunday afternoon, I said, "We're going on a picnic." Danièle asked:

"Where?"

"Miville Grenier's new house. Seems it has to be seen."

My wife gave a whistle when we went in, and my daughter said:

"Wow, it's beautiful here."

My wife asked:

"He's not here, Miville? I don't see his car."

"No, he wanted me to do a bit of inspection."

My wife toured the house. The second floor was still very much a work in progress, but the first was liveable. That's what

I was banking on. She explored the outside too, in a state of bliss. The little one was running all over with the dog. Danièle said:

"They're lucky, Miville and his wife. They're going to have a really beautiful house."

I threw her the keys and I said:

"Just as well, because it's not Miville's house. It's yours."

She looked at me wide-eyed, as if she didn't understand.

"Don't give me that," she said.

"I mean it."

I remember everything after that, but not in order, I remember it like it was all happening at the same time. My wife jumping into my arms, my wife going to get Julie and telling her "It's our house, it's our house!", the dog yapping, everybody running around. She can say whatever she likes, she'll never take that moment away from me. Never mind if my ex now says she found the house too big and too old and it was all wrong because the little one was already scared the very first time she saw it. It's not true. She was happy that afternoon. I was the best husband and father in the world and we were happy, all three of us. And it stayed that way for a while before things really went bad.

It's funny, because I remember Danièle's smile, and Danièle's smell and her taste, I swear, but I can't any more say a kind word about her. I figure I wouldn't speak so badly about her if I hadn't loved her so much. She's gone now, and my little girl's gone, and I'm living in the house with another woman. I don't love it the way I did at the beginning even if today it's my house, my very own house. It's not the same as when I was fixing it up.

Not many people will understand me, but there's something strange about taking over an ancestral domain. This wasn't my first house, but it was the first that made me feel like

I had to wrest it away from somebody. Before I took advantage of the Villeneuves' decline and snapped it up, three generations had lived in the house, never doubting that it was theirs by right. When a man buys a place like that, he buys the nest and protective shell of someone else, someone else's wiring, and someone else's ideas, and he has to decide how far he's going to go to become that person, how much of that man he's prepared to graft onto himself. And there's no getting around it. Two men had inherited the house. From the little I knew, it was Hermenégilde Villeneuve who'd built it at the turn of the century as a summer house for the family, Médéric Villeneuve who'd modernized it and turned it into a principal residence, and Viateur, the artist, who'd let it run down to the point where I was able to buy it.

It was Médéric, in particular, who haunted my thoughts while I was going over his improvements. That he might have delegated many of the jobs to someone else didn't even occur to me. People like me, they hone their skills at an early age on the cabins and then the houses of the men in their family. By the time I'd made my first purchase, there was a lot I could already do. Médéric, it seemed, had learned everything on the job, on just this one site. I could date the work by the differences in quality. The plumbing was impressive, even if it had started acting up in old age. The wiring was done any which way. He'd used newspaper to insulate some of the walls I tore down. I smoothed out the pages to see what was written there. Hardly anyone will believe me, but there was a lot of talk about the Cuban embargo and the Warren Commission. The carpentry was beautiful. The roof had been well built at the time, but Viateur had let it run down.

I worked so much before we moved in and so much after that I hardly noticed the time. I finished the swimming pool and the terracing in the back so my wife could have a place to entertain, but little by little I realized that she was getting tired of living in a construction site. She griped about the water coming out of the faucets either too hot or too cold, she griped about the lights that didn't go on and the bulbs that flickered, she griped about the rooms that were less well insulated than in the old house, and the drafts, she griped about the creaking floors and the knocking pipes. I think she'd always found old houses beautiful without understanding what it was like to live in one, the work it demanded, and the lack of comfort, at least for a while. I suppose it was stupid on my part not to have seen it coming. It was always the same thing with her. We'd bought a cabin in the woods because she thought it would be fun to go there, but we never did go except to make four trips weighed down with supplies so she could be as snug as she was in town, and could ward off flies at all times. One year I rented from a buddy a villa in Venezuela that I'd thought of buying so we could go away every winter, and teach Julie to dive and to speak Spanish. Danièle thought it was the best idea in the world until she saw her first lizard, and realized that the meat was not wrapped in cellophane at the market. Christ, she couldn't even sleep in a four-star hotel—I'm talking about in North America—without bringing along her own pillows, her own shampoo, and a disinfectant for the bathroom. Just to be sure.

The little one was doing okay, I think. Until one night. I was putting the cover over the swimming pool, when I heard her cry out. It had to be almost midnight, and she'd been asleep for about two hours. She cried and then her dog yapped and yapped and I ran to her bedroom. Danièle was already there. The little one was all in a sweat in her bed. The damn dog wouldn't stop barking. I gave it a good kick in the side and that made it yap even more, and my daughter cried even louder. Danièle gave me a black angry look, and said:

"Get out of here, Gilles, get out."

I left. I made myself a big Cutty Sark with lots of ice. Danièle came to join me about an hour later.

"It's all right, she's calmed down. We have to do something, Gilles."

"Something about what?"

"To purify the house. I'm going to ask Jacqueline Martel if she knows someone."

"Will you please tell me what you're talking about?"

"We're seeing things. Your daughter's seeing things."

"Seeing what, for God's sake?"

She looked at me as if I were slightly retarded.

"Ghosts, Gilles. Your bloody old house is full of ghosts."

I tried to stay calm, but I was livid. I must have told her she was crazy over and over again, with lots of bad words mixed in. My wife behaved with her daughter as if she'd been born to be her best friend. She did everything with her, and told her everything. Once, while I was consulting on the Côte-Nord, they'd watched *The Exorcist* together. Holy shit, Julie was nine years old. Danièle had never read a book in her life that didn't talk about past lives, or chakras, or abductions by extraterrestrials, or spontaneous combustion, or women whose children were stolen by Arabs, all that kind of bullshit. A whole library chock full of charlatans and scaremongers. The books were lying around everywhere, and my daughter read them all day long as if they were Tinker Bell fairy tales.

"I've had nothing to do with that, Gilles, I swear."

"Right. Like with Thomas, I suppose."

That had been one of our biggest blow-ups before this particular night. The little one was just four years old. I'd come home from work and given her a bath while reading the newspaper and checking in on her from time to time. She was talking to someone while I wasn't watching her. I noticed that two or three times.

"What's your friend's name, Julie?"

"He's not my friend, he's my little brother. He's called Thomas."

I almost puked. I had to hide myself on the other side of the door, in the hall, so the little one wouldn't see me like that. Thomas was the name my first wife wanted to give to our child. She'd always been sure it would be a boy, and at the hospital they'd confirmed that that was the case. Then we had a car accident on the way home from her parents' in Lac-Saint-Jean. She was twenty-six weeks pregnant. I was driving, and yes, I'd been drinking. But it was another car that hit us because of the freezing rain. It was a pretty bad collision, but no one suffered any serious injuries except for Diane, who had a big bloodstain on her dress. We prayed all the way to the hospital but it didn't help. They removed the dead baby from her belly, and performed a curettage. Diane was half dead too, and I left her there and went back home. I got drunk and I took the baby's room apart with a sledgehammer before putting everything, the clothes, the diapers, the toys, and the hunks of wall, into five big garbage bags. We separated six months later, about the same time I met Danièle. A little after, if you want to know the truth.

When I saw there was nothing magical in all that, I went to talk to Danièle, but she didn't feel bad about it or anything. Back then she'd wanted to have another child. Not me. I figured that just the one had made her crazy enough, the way things stood. She answered me in her curt little tone of voice:

"She had to know that she'd already had a little brother."

I clenched my fists and shut my mouth and waited for her to apologize but she never did, not once, during the seven or eight months that Julie went on calling her imaginary friend by the name of my stillborn son.

I don't want to speak badly of her, but it wasn't just the paranormal and stuff like that. The first time I took her out of her village to my favourite restaurant in Old Quebec, Danièle ordered lobster with a glass of milk. A year after we were married, she called me at my office in a state because she was missing a special kind of salt for the recipe she was making for supper. She wanted me to go and find some, super fast, at the fine foods place in the lower town. I said okay, even if I had a thousand things to do more urgent than that. I picked up a writing pad and asked her what kind of salt she needed.

"Optional salt," she said.

"Are you kidding me, Danièle?"

In her book, it was written "One teaspoon salt (optional)," and she'd spent all morning freaking out over that.

Fine. That's all to say that where good judgment was concerned, my ex-wife was no smarter than a mouse. And as if to prove it, when I asked her that night, "You didn't tell my stories about the house to the little one, did you?" she looked down at the ground as if to say, "You know I did."

There were some very strange things about the house, which I found once I got inside. Two things in particular, that would never have done so much harm, had my ex-wife not blabbed them to a little twelve-year-old girl who had an inordinate fondness for scary stories.

The first week, after I'd signed the act of sale with the Villeneuve son, I took a stroll through the house. There was a horrible smell coming from the basement. The good woman Villeneuve didn't seem to have ventured there very often. I went down the stairs and followed the smell to a padlocked door. I broke off the lock with a screwdriver. That room is where I have my workbench now. When I entered it for the first time, there was nothing there. It was a big cement room without even a naked bulb in the ceiling socket. The smell was dizzying and disgusting. I left to get my flashlight, and went back. I shone the light around until I saw something. There was a cat on the ground, dead for weeks, and eaten by vermin. I got rid of it the next day by peeling it off the ground with a shovel, and I had acid reflux when the body broke in two, letting thick liquid run onto the floor. I never found out what the cat was doing there. In theory, the room was hermetically sealed. Either someone had let it in and locked the door, or else, as cats do at times, it had got in through an improbable opening like a rift in the floor, then in poor condition, and wasn't able to get out again.

Not a big deal, anyway. The second thing I came on later, when I had to open up the attic on the third floor. I hadn't inspected it the first time through because I didn't even know there was a room there. I thought it was just lost space under the roof, but the architect I hired to redo the house found the original plans in the municipal archives. He said there was a room up there. His idea was to renovate the master bedroom upstairs by opening up the floor above it to add height, and gain access to the skylight he saw in the plan. Before starting his design he wanted me to confirm its existence.

In a second-floor room, in the corner, there were two doors that you could easily mistake for cupboards. The second was one in fact, but the first opened onto a small staircase. At the top there was a solid oak door with a large lock on the outside. The key to open it was not on the key ring the Villeneuve son had given me. Nor anywhere else. I got out my chainsaw once more. It was too bad because it was a handsome door, but it was going to disappear in any case, given the architect's plan. I was careful not to fall backwards into the stairway, and I cut a big square out of the door around the lock, which fell to the floor, so all I had to do was push.

The room was just barely illuminated by the light from the opening in the roof. It was humid and musty. It also seemed to smell of pee. The floor was of barnwood, not maple, like in the rest of the house. There were two beds: a small single bed with drawers underneath, almost child size, and a Health Management Systems hospital bed with wooden uprights. There was also a chest of drawers with a little television on top, a wardrobe at the back, and on the right wall the opening for a dumbwaiter that communicated with the kitchen. On the descending walls of the dormered roof, there were posters: Judas Priest, Iron Maiden, and three ladies, boobs in the air. Even where it peaked, in the middle, the room was suffocating. Your instinct was to bend your neck so as not to bump the ceiling, which couldn't have been more than seven feet at its highest point. In the middle of the room, between the two beds, there was a wheelchair.

I couldn't understand their putting a handicapped person's room in such an out-of-the-way corner of the house, where it couldn't have been an easy matter to enter and leave. It was as if the furniture was walled up in there, as well. I had to take the two beds apart to get them out.

The armchair, the cupboard, and the chest of drawers just barely squeaked through. I kept the wardrobe, a lovely cherry wood piece, to refinish it, and all the rest I threw out. Except for the wheelchair, which I brought down to the basement, I don't know why.

Hardly anyone believes me, but under the standard bed someone had carved a symbol like this, with a knife, in the wooden floor:

I didn't want to start in with Villeneuve Junior or Madame in her old folks' home, so instead I went to see Armand Sénécal.

I hadn't seen him for ages, and I'd been told that he was going all over town telling everyone he wasn't overjoyed that I was the one who'd bought the Villeneuve house. He felt he'd been had. That's not exactly the word he used, but never mind. I went to see him in his office downtown, we chewed each other out over it for a while, then I told him I hadn't paid much more for the house than I'd advised him to put into it, and that I had a good ten years ahead of me to renovate it, just like I'd said. I was prepared to do it, he wasn't, and nobody had screwed anyone. He said, "Okay, you're right," and then he asked me what I was doing there. I told him about the room in the attic, and then I asked him if he knew what the story was.

Senecal said:

"When Médéric Villeneuve handed down his house, it was on one condition. Whoever inherited it had to keep on there the two youngest sons in the family. The room at the top was set up for them, they were there during vacations, and then all year round when Médéric moved into the house permanently. There was about three years between them. Vallaire, the older one, was not handicapped, he was just weak in the head. Thibeau, the younger, had Andermann Syndrome. The Charlevoix sickness. After he was twelve or thirteen years old, he could no longer walk. His spine was all twisted with scoliosis, and he had epileptic seizures to boot. From what I heard, he was slow in some ways, for sure, but overall he was a bit more with it than his brother. It's Viateur who took them on, and it's Viateur who got the house. He paid a nurse to take care of them, but I think his wife and children helped out a lot, given that the inheritance was dwindling away. At the end, the nurse came only during the day, when they weren't there. It was a big burden for a small family. Was there ever anything like that in yours?"

"No. What happened to the brothers? They ended up being placed, I imagine?"

"They're dead."

He seemed ill at ease. He must have seen the expression on my face, not at all happy with the news, because he went on:

"Not in your house. But not far away either, I have to say. Do you really not remember the story? It was in 1982, or maybe '83."

"I was working in Montreal then."

"Yes, that's right. Okay. One night when Viateur, his wife, and his children had gone off I don't know where, and the nurse had left as well, the eldest took his little brother in his arms, and carried him down to the main floor. He put him in his wheelchair, pushed him outside, and down along the path that led to the old rock quarry. There was a place where the path turned sharply to the left because in front there was a drop of about a hundred feet leading to a cliff and then to the lake of rainwater that had built up at the bottom of the quarry. Once there, Villaire raised up the chair as though to unload a wheelbarrow, and tipped his brother over the edge. Vallaire then threw himself after him. When the adults got back they found the wheelchair sitting there, and the police retrieved the two brothers from the waterhole the following week. That wasn't a sheer cliff. Their bodies had been torn apart on the rocks as they tumbled down. It seems that they were so mangled when they came out of the water that each body had to be pieced together in order to determine which one was the cripple."

A chill ran down my back. I told myself that I had absolutely to check out that path before Julie hurt herself, playing outside.

"The worst thing about the story is that when you think about it a little, you can understand. Mario Leroux, the guy from the provincial police, talked to me about it one night when we were having a beer at the Le Stade sports bar. He said, 'You know, in that business, there were two problems. Vallaire Villeneuve didn't have all his marbles, but he wasn't crazy enough to do something like that. Thibeau wasn't exactly an Olympic champion, but he wasn't so paralyzed as to have that done to him without at least trying to throw himself to the ground, or something. We didn't tell the papers what we really thought, because we didn't want to hurt anybody. Our conclusion was based on the fact that people with Andermann Syndrome tend to go psychotic. If you ask me, it's Thibeau, who couldn't walk, who convinced his big brother to perform the act. Can you imagine?'"

I could imagine very well. I thanked Armand for the fascinating story, and above all for not having told it to me before. I went home, I pulled the wheelchair out of the basement, and took it right to the dump. The following Sunday I drove to Potvin & Bouchard, to the lumberyard. Back home, I was able to find the old path without clearing it out, I made my way down to the drop-off, I tried not to look at the waterhole staring back at me like a cadaver's eye, and I spent all day building a barrier that's still there, intact.

All that doesn't make for a haunted house. No point losing your head over it. It's horrible enough, but the truth is that going back into the brothers' room that night after having made the barricade, I just felt very sad. I thought about their life in that room. A nothing life, so small in scale that it could make you want to execute a grand, insignificant suicide. I don't know. Along the grapevine it must certainly have seemed a fearful tale, but for me the lives of Vallaire and Thibeau Villeneuve amounted first and foremost to a very sad story. Over the following weeks I took apart the brothers' room under the eaves, and I sent all the wood to the dump. I don't know who Vallaire and Thibeau wanted to hex, carving the devil's sign into the floor, but now the curse is someone else's business.

I was smart enough not to tell the whole story to my ex-wife. When we moved in, all she knew about was the old room and the marks on the floor. That was enough to impress the little one, but at least it wasn't the Stephen King novel cover to cover.

I let two days go by, and then I went to talk to Julie one night, before she went to bed. I was gentle and I tried to reassure her. She asked me if I wanted to see her big notebook. I said "Yes, my lovely." In a Canada notebook, for at least six months, she'd been keeping track of all the strange things going on in the house:

> The dates and hours when her little dog Mélodie yapped *for no good reason*; she who'd howled all the goddam day ever since we'd got her, long before moving in here. Who howled at the clock, at noises in the street, at squirrels, at her shadow.

> The dates and hours when there was *mysterious knocking* in the house, *from inside the walls*; knocking that was no mystery, since some of the plumbing dated from before the war—the First War, I mean to say.

> Sketches indicating the before and after locations of objects that had shifted position in the house. The list included things like the car keys on the table and winter boots in the hall, and I had to stop myself from telling Julie that I knew the cleaning woman was a ghost.

> Entries dated, but with no time, such as *I felt a presence in the TV room*, or as if to enrage me even more, *Mama says she was pushed by a force and almost fell downstairs*. That was dated the Saturday before, when the poltergeist had been able to capitalize on the fact that Danièle was drunk as a skunk after Alain Laganière and his wife had come to have dinner and play cards.

And so on and so forth. For pages and pages.

Most of the entries gave the dates and hours when doors had slammed in the middle of the night. I remember being afraid for her and feeling sorry for her. Poor Julie. Poor us. I remember taking her in my arms like when she was little, and rocking her for a long time. Perhaps I should have come clean then and there, but I decided to let things go.

There were so many slammed doors in those days that it couldn't hurt to blame two or three of them on ghosts.

After that things were better, things were worse, but they were never good any more. My wife and her friend Louise hired some clown with a moustache to *purify the house*: he walked all over mumbling in some bizarre language, and burning cheap incense. My daughter kept on adding to her notebook, but she didn't have any more night sweats, and I suspected her of having begun to draw attention to herself at school with all that stuff. My wife, as she did with anything and everything, used the negative energy on the loose in our household as a pretext to spend money. She had to regain control of the house, she said, and to do so for the family. In practice that meant unloading vast sums onto her decorator friend, buying mountains of knick-knacks and trinkets every day, ordering lamps and furniture from the ends of the earth, then spending almost fifteen thousand bucks to have a made-to-measure feng shui bed built for our room, wide as two king beds, so wide in fact that there was no way we could come into contact except by making a special effort.

The little one thought the house had destroyed our marriage. Danièle must have thought so too because she never disputed anyone who had a stupid idea. But the truth was that it was all over long before we got here. I'll never tell her, but we were done as soon as Julie was born. Everything that wasn't working between us got even worse after that. Danièle was crazy and I was drinking. She liked to take a nip herself, mind you, and I wasn't totally sane either. I suppose we'd be able to admit as much separately today, but certainly not face to face.

After the little one was born, sleeping with my wife became a long-term project. One that never cost me less than a couple of hundred bucks. Danièle began to fear for everything, for herself and for the little one, all the time. Nothing I did made any sense to her. We also had a different way of dealing with the fact that the business was doing well and I was making money. She came from a small village where she'd always held her own because of her beauty, and now she loved playing the parvenu, looking down her nose at her brothers and sisters, all of whom hated me because I'd turned her into a snob. But I came from the lower town, where you can get hammered for lots of reasons, but never harder than for a swelled head. I like paying for a round and buying big cars, but never in a hundred years would I go on about it, talking with my mouth all puckered up as did my wife, who came off as a real turkey, articulating like a countess with her three-hundred-word vocabulary.

I suppose it was partly my fault, because I spoiled her. I always liked letting her spend money so people could see what I had without my needing to make a big deal of it myself. When Julie was born, I had the same reflex as lots of workers' sons: I wanted to close the floodgates so my daughter wouldn't be the most coddled baby in the world. So she wouldn't turn into a rich kid I couldn't even talk to. I don't know. All I know is that there was no way I could raise my daughter old-style with her mother taking herself for Empress Sisi right alongside. But there, at least, things worked out. She's tough today, my daughter. She earns her own money and she's not scared of anyone, but I'm not liar enough to say it's thanks to me.

By the time we moved into the house, things had already gone sour. We made love about ten times a year. I tried to reconcile myself to that because we'd almost divorced in 1987 after my affair with a secretary. So I drank a lot, and yes, I was in a foul humour most of the time. Since Danièle was afraid of everything, and refused to go for counselling and said it was me who was crazy and irresponsible, the only place to spend our money was at the shopping centre. We didn't travel any more because every country in the world was too dangerous for the little one—except for the States and Walt Disney World, which a normal guy soon gets tired of visiting. It was a real problem going to a restaurant because my wife ate nothing and was always scared that the people in the kitchen had left the chicken on the counter more than five minutes, or touched the meat with their bare hands. I tried to start a wine collection but she said it was stupid to pay fifty bucks for bottles that really aren't any better than those you can get for ten, and anyway it was just another reason to get drunk.

Danièle babied our daughter and you couldn't talk to her about it without her jumping all over you. She overprotected her and spoiled her and at the same time overexposed her by telling her all sorts of nonsense about men in general and me in particular. At one point she was reading another one of her ladies' books: *The Manipulators Are Among Us*. She made a point of leaving it all over the house with a big bookmark sticking out of it. One afternoon I picked it up and opened it to the page she'd marked. It was the list of "what makes a manipulator":

He makes other people feel guilty in the name of family ties, friendship, love, professionalism;

He holds others responsible, and not himself;

He does not clearly communicate his demands, his needs, his feelings and opinions;

He often gives vague answers;

He alters his opinions, his behaviour, his feelings, to suit different people and situations;

He draws on logic to disguise his own demands;

He makes others believe they must be perfect, must never change their minds, must know about everything, and must respond instantly to his demands and queries;

He calls into question the qualities, competence, character of others: he criticizes without appearing to, puts people down and judges them;

He sends messages via other individuals;

He sows discord and creates suspicion, divides to conquer;

He knows how to portray himself as a victim in order to attract sympathy;

He ignores requests even if he claims to be dealing with them;

He enlists the moral principles of others to satisfy his own needs;

He uses veiled threats, or overt blackmail;

He abruptly changes the subject in the midst of a conversation;

He avoids or walks out on conversations and meetings;

He claims others are ignorant, and proclaims his own superiority;

He lies;

He makes false statements in order to worm out the truth;

He's egocentric;

He can be jealous;

He cannot tolerate criticism and denies evidence;

He doesn't take into consideration the rights, needs, and desires of others;

He often waits until the last minute to give orders to others or to have them act;

His reasoning seems logical or coherent, while his attitudes do not;

He flatters you to please you, offers gifts, will without notice do anything for you;

He generates a feeling of unease or of not being free;

He is very effective in attaining his own goals, but at the expense of others;

He has people do things they would probably not have done of their own free will;

He is constantly the topic of conversations, even when he's not present.

She'd underlined almost everything. I couldn't talk to her about it right away, because that evening we were entertaining her friend Monique and her retard husband.

The same night, I waited for her in bed with her book in hand, and I asked:

"Danièle, will you be so kind as to tell me who you know that's such an asshole?"

She gave me her pinched little snobby look, as if I were the most pathetic case on earth.

"Gilles, it's obvious. That's all about you."

Danièle had magical powers: she could make me furious even when she said exactly what I thought she was going to say. I remember punching the wall, hard, and asking her at the top of my voice if they were going to bring out a second volume to talk about women who were fucking liars and fucking parasites.

We heard Julie crying. Danièle called me a bloody mad-man and then did what she usually did. She took the little one and went off to Quebec City for the weekend. To her sister's. That was something else I could never figure out about her, her being able to persuade herself that she was protecting her daughter by loading her into a car to drive for two hours when she was halfway drunk.

I stayed on alone with the yapping dog and old quarrels sus-pended in air along with the Villeneuve family's ancient dra-mas. That's the weekend something happened in the house, the only thing I could never explain to my daughter.

*

We talked on the phone two or three times in the course of the weekend, Danièle and me. I don't even remember what I said. It was just a ritual, a penance I had to perform every time, so Danièle could get up on her high horse. I promised to be careful. I said that maybe we'd go for counselling somewhere. Above all, I didn't raise my voice once during the calls. The girls came back Monday while I was at work. When I showed up, Danièle and Julie were outside. Danièle stayed on the lawn, while Julie came up to hug me, and asked:

"Papa, have you seen Mélodie?"

"Mélodie? I tied her up outside this morning. Maybe I brought her in, too. She's not in the house?"

"No."

We searched around a bit, calling her name. While Julie wasn't looking, I mimed to her mother over her shoulder my taking a swig from a bottle, and I shrugged my shoulders. In fact, I hadn't seen the dog since Sunday. The little one was concerned. At supper we reassured her, telling her that the dog had perhaps run away. That papa had maybe forgotten to close the patio door at one point, it had been hot over the weekend. After three days, my wife began to wonder whether the dog had been hit by a car.

I printed up flyers at the office, with a photo of the dog and our telephone number on it. We went to put it up all over the neighbourhood, once Julie got home from school. There were no calls. We began to tell the little one that Mélodie must be dead. She was ten years old, after all. Maybe she'd got sick. Maybe she'd decided to go and hide in the woods to die.

On Saturday I was at my workbench in the basement, when Julie came to find me. She said:

"Papa, I'd like to show you something while mama's not here."

"Right away?"

"Yes. I think I found Mélodie."

I took off my goggles and put them down on the sawhorse. "I'm with you, my lovely," I said, and we went outside. We walked out behind the swimming pool, to the edge of the woods. Julie rooted around in the branches a little, before saying, "It's here." A chill went down my back when I saw that she'd found the path leading to the old Villeneuve rock quarry. We walked up to the barrier I'd built almost two years earlier. The little one leaned out over it. "Be careful," I said. "Don't worry," she replied. "Don't worry, just look."

Down below there was something in the hole. The body of a little disjointed animal afloat in the black water, black as well, but another, duller, black. I took a deep breath, and then I asked:

"Julie, I promise you that we'll go see if it's Mélodie. Over on the other side, though, because the path gets dangerous here. But first I want you to tell me why you came here."

"No, I don't want to."

"Julie. Tell me."

"Because it's the lake where Thibeau and Vallaire Villeneuve died."

I shut my eyes and clenched my fists and I felt Julie clinging to me.

"Papa, listen to me. It's not mama who told me, I swear. It's that big Christine at school. Don't be mad, papa. Don't be mad."

We went back to the house to pick up gloves and a shovel and a big burlap bag. We took my car and went round by the old town. The quarry's blocked-off entry gave onto a little road bordering the Saguenay, gloomy as it always was on a cloudy day. I pried the padlock off the gate with a crowbar, and we went in. We threw rocks into the water until Mélodie washed up on shore. I told Julie to look away.

We buried her behind the swimming pool shed that night. The little one was sad for about a week. After that she calmed down, and the whole house grew calm as well.

As if it had accepted a sacrifice.

Things went on that way for a while. My wife decorated and decorated. The house quickly turned into a labyrinth of little pedestal tables and shelves and tiny end tables with little knick-knacks and little lamps on top and little feet underneath. Dozens of goddam little feet to stub your little toe on in the dark at four in the morning. My daughter made note of every creaking door and every wailing pipe, in her book of mysteries. She took dozens of Polaroids. Photos of nothing. She took them against the light or in complete darkness until she had one strange enough to paste into her notebook. She dyed her hair black and put on black lipstick and she seemed on her way to buying all the black clothes her size in the whole world. I remember saying to myself, "Christ, if she could only get interested in boys a little." I remember regretting that a lot when the tomcats started circling her, later on.

My wife had finally decided not to move our bedroom upstairs. She said she wasn't comfortable sleeping on a different floor from her anxious daughter. So I decided to renovate, building apartments overhead, along with Denis Harvey, Alain Laganière, and Yvon Bouchard. That kept me busy for a few months. We worked hard at night and on weekends. Sometimes we ordered in Saint-Hubert barbecue instead of going downstairs. My wife never seemed happy cooking us supper, in any case. And sometimes we ended the day a bit drunk and I let the guys go, saying "I'm going to clean up a bit," then I watched them through the big front windows, taking off in their cars, and I lay down there, right on the floor, with my shirt rolled up into a ball for a pillow. I was never in a rush to leave the construction site, with its good smell of beer and wood shavings, just to go and join my frigid wife in her giant bed.

One Tuesday, I had to go to Lac-Saint-Jean to inspect a factory in Chambord. I asked Danièle if she wanted me to cancel. "No, that's fine, go ahead," she said. "I'll take care of the little one."

I had a feeling something wasn't quite right.

When I got back three days later, the girls were gone.

It took two weeks for Danièle to tell me where they were. With her sister in Quebec City, obviously. They'd be coming back, but not to the house. She'd take an apartment because she needed to think. That apartment, I helped her find it, I painted it, and I paid for it for six months. I'm just saying. I went to pick up Julie twice a week to go to a restaurant and then a movie. She didn't want to sleep at the house any more. Neither of them talked to me much about the dog, afterwards. Either they'd mourned for it normally, or they knew I wouldn't be a good audience for their paranormal theories. Meanwhile, I'd finished the lodgings on the second floor, and put tenants into them. And no one ever complained about anything, including the mother and daughter who lived in the apartment where Thibeau's and Vallaire's room used to be.

I put up with my wife's little fit of independence for almost a year. Until people in town began telling me there was another man in the picture. Over the telephone, I asked her to explain.

"I don't know if it's serious with that man, but you really don't seem to want to change, Gilles."

"What do you want?" I asked. "I'd like us to get along but I don't know what you want."

"I think for starters, you'd have to acknowledge your drinking problem, and sell the goddam house."

"Yes, but you, what are you ready to do to put things back on track?"

"What do you want me to do, Gilles? I'm not the one who's sick."

I saw red. The little voice in my head told me to shut up, but I opened my trap anyway:

"I'm going to tell you something, my lovely, and you can put that in your pipe. I'm always going to drink because I like to drink and anyway there's no man in the world who could put up with a goddam crazy woman like you and still be on the wagon. And I'll never give up my house. Never."

I hung up. Maybe she called back but I wouldn't have known because I completely destroyed the phone, slamming down the receiver. It took ten years before we saw each other without lawyers being present.

★

Today Julie's almost thirty. She has two little girls and a husband. They're in Montreal. I would have liked them to stay in the area, but what can you do? Since she left for Montreal at the age of nineteen, she's come to see me every time she's been back to the Saguenay, but she never wants to stay long in the house, and not once has she slept there more than one night. Yesterday, the whole family arrived together. I talked with my son-in-law, who I don't know very well, the older girl spent all day in the swimming pool, while the smaller one, who's not even a year, amused herself in her baby saucer in the shade under a big umbrella. At night we put the girls to bed and ate outside, all four of us, my wife, my daughter, my son-in-law, and me, with crab claws on the barbecue.

It was a really nice day.

We ate like pigs and laughed and my daughter even told some stories out of her adolescence, and then letting her go on, as though nothing were up, I went in to get her mystery notebook. She gave a yelp when I showed it to her, all embarrassed. We talked about knocks in the wall from the plumbing, floors that squeaked, and blurred photos. Still, at one point she said:

"You can laugh, but you never found an explanation for the dog."

"Ah, your Mélodie... she must have fallen, what can I tell you?"

My wife didn't know the story, so Julie told it to her. After that I changed the subject, as usual. I said, "You didn't know, eh, Roxanne, that you lived in a haunted house?" I made myself laugh and told them that Roxanne thought there was a vampire in the basement, an evil creature but not really nasty, a kind of spirit who bled the life out of people's veins, bite by bite. I even had a friend who taught at the University of Quebec and wanted to interview her about it because he'd never heard of people believing in vampires anywhere else but in Eastern Europe and the Balkans.

*

That time when Danièle took off to Quebec City with my daughter, and when Mélodie disappeared, I didn't sober up much for the entire weekend. I don't recall everything, but I do remember pacing up and down in the house having imaginary arguments with my wife, and I remember ripping a lot of shelves off the wall and throwing all kinds of stuff onto the floor, and having to pick it all up on Sunday. Saturday night I went to bed early with a big headache.

About ten o'clock, the dog started to yap. I came out of the bedroom and found it sitting right in the middle of the living room, head in the air, barking at nothing. It lay down when it saw me coming. I petted it a little, talking softly, and it followed me into the bed. It didn't stay for long. I felt it steal off, and half asleep, I heard it, from time to time, coming out with its big dumb yaps.

From when she was born to the age of eleven, more or less, my daughter had her Jack. He was a German shepherd mixed up with all sorts of other things. I'd picked him out of a farm dog's litter, at Saint-Coeur-de-Marie. My daughter was still in her mother's womb. Julie and Jack had been a great love story. We often stayed in the country when my daughter was little, so that Jack was her constant companion. Even later, when we were living on city streets where there were more children, she often preferred to stay all alone with Jack.

Two weeks after Jack's death, my wife turned up with a little miniature schnauzer. "The best little dog in the world," she said. A friend had given it to her, neglecting to mention that it yapped with all its might at the drop of a hat. She didn't especially like dogs, my ex-wife, and in fifteen years of cohabitation, I don't think I saw her scooping up droppings more than five times. But she had the firm belief that for a child, life without a dog was no life at all, and it would require another mutt for Julie to be consoled. I'm not sure that was true, and I would have preferred her to consult me beforehand, at the very least. I'm the one who'd trained Jack, and I'd kept him groomed, and I'd had him immunized, and to tell the truth I could have used a little dog break before taking on another.

Mélodie really had no chance with me. I didn't much like that dog. Her yapping didn't help, for sure, especially after my wife and daughter had started using it as evidence for there being something wrong with our house.

In short, I disliked the dog, and it got on my nerves more and more when it started howling its head off. I went down mad as hell to the living room and delivered it a good big kick in the side. I never liked hitting dogs, but for a long time, with her, I hadn't been able to restrain myself. She got up and came in between my legs while continuing to yip at the top of her lungs. I chased her all through the house, and she ended up making one bad move, crossing in front of the staircase leading to the basement. I was right behind her and was able to give her another kick in the side that sent her tumbling down the stairs.

I went down after her very slowly. The dog was making high-pitched noises. She tried crawling again but I whomped her with my foot a third time, hard, and now I heard bones crack. She peed on the cement floor from fear, and lay down in submission. I grabbed her by the neck. I could say that I was mad or possessed by the twin devil of Vallaire and Thibeau Villeneuve, but I won't say that. Because it's not true. I didn't see red and I didn't see black. My anger was white, and everything was perfectly clear in my head. I wasn't even drunk. That was the most terrible moment, when I understood in the same instant that I could stop, but that I wouldn't, because in every fibre I was serene in what I was doing. The dog wriggled around. I shook it one way and then the other, and when I had a good grip, I squeezed with all my strength. Men in the past invented spirits, vampires, and werewolves, so as to accuse them of crimes they committed themselves, and I was no better than them, no better than anyone. It wasn't a spirit or a demon that killed Mélodie, it was just me. Me, my madness, and my bare hands.

I left the dog there with its tongue sticking three inches out of its mouth, and its eyes almost popping out of their orbits. I went to bed, and the next day, when I woke up with the sun, to fumes of alcohol, I was able not to think about it for at least ten minutes. Then it came back, and I told myself that the old quarry would be a good place to get rid of the body. I walked there carrying the dog in front of me, letting the branches and thorns scratch at my bare arms and face, and I heaved it down without even glancing at it one last time.

I never told anyone and I'll always deny it. My wife and my daughter have brought up the subject a lot, but each time I've said "The dog fell in the hole, give me a break with that." You may think I'm making a confession by telling this story, but it's not true. I've changed it just enough that no one will know me, and if by some stroke of bad luck my daughter recognizes me anyway, I'll say, "Are you crazy?"

I'll always deny having done it, and I'd give the same advice to any man who perpetrates a similar abomination. Deny it to your dying day. Swear on the head of your parents, swear on the head of your wife, swear on the head of anyone except your children, and swear on their heads too if you have no choice. Invent a story, tell a pack of lies, put a curse on your eternal soul, but for the love of God keep your mouth shut.

★

Something odd happened yesterday. Julie slept in the house, and in the morning, she found nothing strange. Her eldest had woken in the night after a nightmare, and she'd made a big commotion, and her father had had to put her back to sleep, but this morning my daughter didn't say it was the fault of the house, or of Thibeau and Vallaire, or I don't know what. We ate breakfast together outside, it was a lovely morning. Roxanne and I are leaving on vacation the day after tomorrow, so just like that I said, "Hey, if you want you can take the house for the week with the girls. Our pleasure."

I waited for Julie to burst out laughing. But she and her guy looked at each other, normally, and then she said:

"We'll think about it, papa. It's true this would make a super place for us to stay when we're in the Saguenay."

I couldn't believe it. I was really happy. Just in case, in the afternoon, I showed my son-in-law how to put the solar blanket on the swimming pool, how to work the heat pump and the retractable awning on the terrace, and the outside sound system if they wanted to put some music on. I showed him my wine cellar and my meat freezer in the basement, saying "Don't be shy, eh, it's our pleasure."

Then I added:

"In any case, if you can convince my daughter to sleep here for a week, I'll tip my hat to you. Even now, she's still thinks there are supernatural things going on in the house."

He looked at me, my son-in-law, then he said with an odd little smile, a bit mysterious:

"Oh, I think that you too, you saw some strange things back then."

He brought me up short, I confess. I didn't stick my neck out, or anything. I just said, to shut him up:

"Yes, it's true. I've seen things. But they had nothing to do with the house."

I almost added something else, but I decided to leave things there. We looked at each other in silence, and we understood each other. And I gave him the last word, even if that's not like me.

"Don't worry, everything's cool now. Julie's a lot calmer. And anyway, with houses like yours, you get what you put in."

I like him fine, that boy. I think my daughter's good with him, and their children are well brought up. I think he's got his head screwed on right, and that what he said is probably the smartest thing you can say about my house, and lots of other things.

You get back what you put in.

Madeleines
ARVIDA III

Once, only once, my grandmother, mother of my father, said:

"There are no thieves in Arvida, Georges. It has to be somewhere."

I was nine or ten years old, and I didn't know what they were talking about. Next to the TV room, in the basement, there was a storage room with an old jumble of things and an oil furnace that leaked, a work bench, and a toilet my brother and I were scared stiff of using for our needs. Doubtless to take pre-emptive action against any impending adolescent onanism, my grandmother said that if you sat there for too long, the odour of young flesh and excrement could lure a voracious rat into the pipe.

Georges had been rooting around in there for two days when he finally cried out, "Eureka!" He and my grandmother called me alone into the middle of the clutter. On a table as small as a sewing machine stand, Georges had placed a different kind of machine: black, with a keyboard in front, a white page slipped in over a roller and up through a kind of target in the middle of the sheet, held in place by a metal rod mounted on a mechanism set between the two extremities of a red and black ribbon. Above the keyboard, below the machine's big opening where the type bars were all lined up like organ pipes, was inscribed in big letters:

UNDERWOOD

My grandfather had bought the typewriter just after the war, at a time when, with the European economy only slowly getting back on its feet, Quebec had become Underwood's best market for, at a discount, unloading its backlog of machines with French keyboards.

To make ends meet, my grandfather and grandmother had used it to write articles for *Progrès-Dimanche* and later for *La Source*. On this machine, all my aunts and uncles had worn out their fingernails and joints in the course of their studies. On this machine my grandfather had written, all his life long, scouting reports for the Chicago Blackhawks, the New York Rangers, and at the Junior level, the Quebec Remparts. What is more, on this machine he'd said for the first time that Michel Goulet, a young left-winger from Péribonka, would be a gold mine for any club that got its hands on him.

Georges had oiled and greased it, and it was like new.

This was in 1988 or 1989, however, and I didn't quite know what they wanted me to do with their antique. My grandmother explained:

"It's for your stories."

"What stories?"

"The ones you're telling all the time. And the ones you make up."

It's true that at that age I was a bit of a liar. In fact, since I was very young, I'd tended to exasperate my brother and his friends by forcing on our little toys (G.I. Joe, He-Man, and the Playmobil characters) lengthy melodramas, before letting them throw a single punch.

"Those stories, exactly. You could write them on this, and they wouldn't bother anybody. Besides, you'd practise your French. And maybe one day they'd be good enough for you to read them to your mother, your father, or me."

I thought that was a good idea. So I quickly familiarized myself with the keys and the mechanics and the gummy letters that sometimes got stuck to the page. I began to recount any old thing on it, especially stories stolen from Will Eisner (whose *Spirit* we had in translation in my uncles' old *Pilote* magazines which my grandmother had saved), and from Stephen King, the world's coolest writer at the time. I wrote awful stories set in an Arvida that wasn't entirely fictional, where the sheriff was called Jim, his wife Deborah, and their son Timothy.

(It's also then that I became an insomniac for good. The child starts to write by resisting sleep. In his room, between the sheets, he wards off what will soon escape him forever, when his whole life he'll be chasing after sleep and feeling it slip through his fingers. But that's where it begins: a child in his bed, in flight from it. Not to sleep, not to dream, never to close his eyes. Darting them everywhere in the darkness, remembering the day, imprinting in his mind everything about it that was ugly and everything that was beautiful.)

Later, I wanted to write my own stuff.

In a little notebook, I jotted things down that I afterwards transcribed onto the machine. I looked into things that had really happened in Arvida, and I tried to put together a kind of working-class mythology. Strange happenings were few and far between, because the town was young and its occult underside pretty tenuous. I listened for stories told by older brothers and sisters that were not silly tales off a Ouija Board or yarns about a demented baby-sitter who roasted babies in an oven like turkey.

I didn't find much.

My mother said that my godmother had once lived in a house in Saint-Mathias where there had been a suicide, and left after a few months, refusing ever to talk about it.

In a house on Rue Faraday, on the second floor, behind a high narrow window giving onto the church, you could see at sundown, in the summer, and when the night sky turned opaque in winter, a woman gazing out distractedly, humming a lullaby to her child. In the bed, the baby was dead. It was a ghost, of course, but the ghost of a dead baby. It wasn't its own ghost, it was part of what was left behind by its dead mother. The baby cried no more, breathed no more, neither in this world nor the next. It was the ghost of something else, something deathly pale, black around the eyes and black at the lips, which the mother was trying to put to sleep. I didn't know if the baby changed. Someone had told me that the baby in the bed was dead. I promised not to say who. Me, on the sidewalk, I just saw the mother bent over the cradle. I'm not even sure she was dead.

On Rue Oersted, a former tenant talked to me about something strange. There were no ghosts at that address. It was just that in a big empty house, you heard, two or three times a year, an echo of ancient conversations. The tenant, alone, intrigued, got up in the middle of the night to check out all the rooms, one by one, in the dark. He had to conclude that those voices came from nowhere.

In the woods stretching from the water purification factory road to the golf course, there lived a monster. When we took that road to get a Pepsi and chips paid for by friends of my father who drank at the clubhouse there, we often heard it, enormous, moving among the branches. We fled, screaming, until we were out of breath and the thick greenery opened out onto the golf course parking lot. I always thought it was a Tyrannosaurus. My brother said it was a werewolf. Stéphane Blais said it was a bear, Jean-Nicolas Frigon a flying shark, and my Bergeron cousins a dragon. Much later, after I'd forgotten the absolute terror and the imagined silhouette that rustled in the leaves, a friend told me that there really was a monster living on the golf course, she'd seen it, and it had told her things.

It was a man.

I tried to write a whole story, once, about our house at the end of Rue Gay-Lussac. It was a huge white wooden house with black shutters, an annex, a double garage, and an inground swimming pool, the dream house my parents had bought when they were rich.

My story was that of a man who as an adult bought back a house he'd lived in as a child. He moved into it with his wife and child, and realized that the house was haunted by himself. The man had been clinically dead at the age of twelve, drowned in the pool. I never managed to finish it, because I didn't know if it was a sad story or a horror story. We'd had to vacate the house in 1987. At the end my parents each slept in their own room at either end of the hall, and the damaged swimming pool had become a real swamp. Frogs swam in its stagnant water, and every week we found dead animals there.

She'd had a good idea, sitting me down in front of the Underwood, my grandmother, mother of my father. Unfortunately for her, and above all for me, there are always times when I get attached to stories that aren't stories really, that begin without ending and never get anywhere. Possibilities, dreams, and missed rendezvous. Phantoms and absences.

My favourite story happened to a friend of my brother, whom I'll just call D.

D. lived alone with his brother and his mother. He talked about how, when he was seven years old, he'd been told his father had died from cancer. This was false, we knew, as D. himself learned later on.

His father had killed himself, jumping from the Shipshaw Bridge.

An engineering jewel financed by Arthur Vining Davis, completed in 1950, opened by Maurice Duplessis, and still today the only aluminum bridge in the world, the Shipshaw Bridge, built in an arc, rises over an arm of the Saguenay River almost forty metres above a dizzying gorge, a rough current, and sharp rocks. I forget how many people actually killed themselves there, but in my father's unfettered imagination, they're legion.

That's also his way of telling me that his morale is low. Sometimes I call, I ask him how he is, and he replies:

"They're serving number 6 on the Shipshaw Bridge. I'm 72."

Many or not, D.'s father was one of them. After D.'s mother had left Arvida for a neighbouring town, she preferred the expurgated story of a cancer to that of suicide.

At the age of sixteen, D. began to go out with a young woman whose family had just resettled in the area, after the father, who worked for Hydro Quebec, had been for two decades posted in various parts of the province. Through his girlfriend, D. learned that his new father-in-law had once been a close friend of his own father.

There came the day when she introduced him to her parents. The usual conversation, silences, unease and forced laughter, until D. finished the beer he'd been offered, and began to feel more at ease. The father was left alone with him, and inquired about his mother, his brother, and himself. After a while, feeling more at ease himself, he asked:

"Do you have news from your father from time to time?"

D. replied, troubled:

"Sir, my father has been dead for ten years."

The father-in-law choked on his beer, and apologized for his unpardonable lapse. They went to the table, but D. had clearly seen how the father had gone pale in pronouncing those words, and how he'd avoided his gaze afterwards. He didn't do anything in front of his girlfriend, and waited for the next day to go and pursue the subject at the man's workplace.

"Sir, yesterday you asked me if I'd had news of my father, and you nearly passed out when I told you he was dead. I'd like to know why. I'd like you to tell me the truth, and not try to make me believe that it was nothing, because I saw in your face that it isn't nothing.

His father-in-law sighed.

"As you wish, my boy. I didn't know your father was dead, because I was far from here at that time. I thought your parents were divorced. But I think you should make your own inquiries, because I ran into your father in the street in Rouyn last year."

Even if I still, today, have a lot of sympathy for D., I'm even more enamoured of the abyss opened up by that reply.

Was it possible that D.'s father wasn't dead?

Had they actually found his body under the Shipshaw Bridge?

I left for Montreal before my brother could tell me the rest, if there was any more to tell. I often, from afar, thought about this mystery, like a fat detective in the pages of a yellowed crime novel.

The most plausible solution I found was that there had been a case of mistaken identity before the meal. D. was not an extremely common family name in the Saguenay, like Tremblay, Girard, or Bouchard, but it wasn't rare either. It was perfectly possible that what with the rumour mill and distant memories, his father-in-law had imagined that D. was the son of a D. who was not his father.

That explained the reappearance. It also explained how a man who claimed to be an old friend, and who had maintained close ties in the region so as to eventually return there, could have utterly failed to hear about the death notice.

Of course, that dispensed with the misunderstanding at the expense of the story. On the other hand, you could invent hundreds of stories and as many different fathers for D., to compound the problem. You could invent for him a fraudster father on the run, a gangster father turned Crown witness, a spy father, an amnesiac father, a father abducted by extra-terrestrials, a father in the Foreign Legion, a homosexual father prey to a blackmailer, a serial killer father, an alcoholic or drug addict father, or, my favourite, an amateur existentialist who had vanished from view and founded elsewhere a new family just like his old one, to put his personal freedom to the test.

On the one hand I'm doing away with the mystery by providing a lacklustre ending. On the other I'm appropriating it and reducing it to nothing through the practice of fiction (and facile fiction, to boot). To tell the story is already to rob it of its power and fascination. For me it all ends just where it began, with the disclosure of a return from the dead that gives rise to an abundance of hypotheses, but none so presumptuous as to shine a glaring light onto this ghostly marvel.

Nothing made writing more difficult for me than this fundamental impossibility. Like the anti-madeleines of my father in which all memory is swallowed up, the stories I like are untellable, or suffer from being told, or self-destruct in the very act of being formulated.

I once talked about this to my father.

We were at a fishing camp in the Valin Mountains.

In the dark, outside, there were insects and animals and plants to which the moon had lent a different colour than what was theirs in the light of day. In the beam of a gas lamp, in the light, there were only the two of us, my father and me.

It was late, and we were two-thirds of the way through a bottle of Johnnie Walker. As was usual in such circumstances, my father wanted me to explain to him things I was too drunk to elucidate. This time he was asking me questions about writing. He wanted to know why I sometimes arrived with my baggage full of bits of stories and beginnings of novels, and why sometimes, for long years, I didn't write a line. I said:

"It's not as easy as that."

"What's so hard? I know thousands of stories. If I could write I'd write all the time."

"Yes, but you wouldn't know so much about it if you spent your time reading other people's books."

"People who know stories can't write them, and people who can write them don't have enough stories. It's not fair."

"I know lots of stories. It's not that that stops me."

"What then?"

"It's telling them that's the problem. I can never find a way to put what I want into the stories."

"I don't understand."

"You know Proust?"

"French author of *In Search of Lost Time*. Six letters."

"Right. That thing there is an Everest. Something like four thousand pages. In it, the narrator tastes a madeleine at the beginning, and that brings back all his childhood memories. Can you imagine? The guy got a whole world out of a cookie."

"A madeleine is not really a cookie."

"I know. But I don't have anything close to that. I have no madeleine. All we wanted, when we were kids, was McDonald's."

"I remember. The kids' games outside and the smell of French fries in the car."

"And McNuggets. I feel like all our stories end at the table, rather than start there. The only story that comes back to me from taking a bite of something has to do with a mouthful of McNugget. I was ten years old, and we were celebrating my birthday in the basement of McDonald's in Jonquière, in the children's room. I took a bite out of a McNugget, and Julie

Morin asked me to give her the rest. At the age of ten, offering her the chewed up half of a McNugget was like offering her an engagement ring, or something like that. I was head over heels in love with her. I blushed, and held out the McNugget to her, and she smiled at me."

"Did she eat it?"

"She didn't have time. There were ladders on the ceiling, you remember? Laurent-Pierre Brassard was like a monkey on them. There was something intoxicating about walking like that on the ceiling, but playing the monkey, he'd got tired. He was just over us when his fingers slipped on the rung of a ladder. Before Julie could take her McNugget, Laurent-Pierre fell on top of us, and there was food everywhere, tables overturned, and pop on the floor. Julie Morin cried, and our engagement was off."

"Is all that true?"

"I'd be surprised. Honestly, after a while you can't tell a real story from an invented one any more, but I know that's all the literature I'll ever get out of a McNugget. And that's where I always end up. McNuggets aren't madeleines, forgetting trumps memory, and you can't write all your life about how hard it is to tell a story."

"Why not?"

I shrugged my shoulders. My father sighed deeply, as if to say "You're complicated, you young people." He went to get us each a beer from the old Coke cooler, to wash down the scotch. While he was shutting the door, his face lit up. He began to tap on his temple with his fingers, which resonated on his skull like on wood, a favourite ploy of his when he wanted you to know there was something going on inside.

"You forget one thing, coco."

"What?"

"Your grandmother."

"Éliane?"

"No. My mother."

"What?

"Her name was Madeleine."

For an instant, I thought about the Sophie cakes that Mado made with sugar and cream that never set, the banana bread, the little squares of white cake on which she poured boiling hot butterscotch and a dribble of cream. I thought of the hares my grandfather skinned himself in the garage, and that my grandmother cooked like an Indian. I thought of a million things, but above all of Mado herself, her smell, her voice, her smile and her tiny eyes behind thick lenses. With those memories came the memories of dozens of stories I could tell, one way or another, or any old way if necessary.

Stories of Arvida and elsewhere.

Horrible stories and funny stories and stories both horrible and funny.

Stories of road trips, little thieves, and people weak in the head.

Stories of monsters and haunted houses.

Stories of bad men, as men often are, and mysterious and terrifying women, as women always are.

True stories I'd tell without asking permission or changing any names, while giving dates and the names of streets.

Terrible stories that I'd never tell except by removing them to the opposite end of the world, or disguising them in strange language.

They all jostled together, taking their time, until I succumbed to the overwhelming fatigue of a day in the open air. There was no hurry. I hugged my father, I pissed outside, and I went to bed early for once, happy to know so many stories.

Beginning with that one.

About the Author

PHOTO BY: FREDERICK DUCHESNE

SAMUEL ARCHIBALD was born in Arvida, Quebec, in 1978. He earned a doctorate at the Université du Québec à Montréal, where he currently teaches creative writing and popular culture. From 2007 to 2009, Archibald was a post-doctoral fellow at the Université de Poitiers, France.

Arvida won two literary prizes and has been universally acclaimed as one of the major works of fiction published in French Canada in recent years. In addition to *Arvida*, Archibald is the author of a novella, and of non-fiction books about reading in the digital age and the decline of the middle class.

About the Translator

DONALD WINKLER is a Montreal-based literary translator and documentary filmmaker. He has translated French language fiction, non-fiction, and poetry for many years, and is a three-time winner of the Governor General's Award for French-to-English translation, most recently, in 2013, for Pierre Nepveu's collection of verse, *The Major Verbs*.